Seducing Jane Porter

Being bad never felt so good...

After being jilted by her former master, Jane Porter looks to end her year-long celibacy by attending a bondage-themed event. Thanks to her ex-boyfriend's stunning betrayal, she isn't looking for happily-ever-after, just a master who's willing to explore the depths of her passion and teach her what the BDSM lifestyle is all about.

Antonio Villareal was a wanted man. Single, rich and good looking, he's on the hunt for a submissive to share his world. The moment he sees Jane on the arm of another man, he wants to possess her body and soul. The only problem is; Jane makes it clear she isn't a forever kind of girl.

Can Antonio convince Jane to give him a chance?

Warning: Graphic sex, bondage scenes and the use of masks.

Educating Jane Porter

He's throwing a kink—or two—in her plans...

Last night Jane met the Master of her dreams...

Tall, dark and very Spanish, Antonio Villareal is a lover unlike any Jane has ever known—undeniably sexy and more than willing to help her explore her submissive side. To find a master who's a natural dominant is one thing. But kind and considerate, as well? She can hardly believe her good fortune.

Antonio is well aware that Jane is determined to keep their sexual relationship temporary. But he has a different plan in mind.

In the morning he introduces her to his best friend...

Warning: This book contains copious amounts of champagne, kinky under-the-table hi-jinks, a ménage to die for, voyeurism and angry shower sex. What more could you want?

Reinventing Jane Porter

Her darkest fantasies are about to come true...

Jane's weekend of mind-blowing sex is drawing to a close. Only one event remains—a masquerade ball. Her masters, Antonio and Santos, will be her escorts, but the party isn't the only item on their agenda. They plan to show her what it really means to live the life of a prized submissive.

After tasting the heady decadence of true sexual freedom, Jane wonders if she can ever go back to her everyday life—or if Beauty will, finally and permanently, be freed from her shell.

Then there's the issue of a former lover lurking in the wings...

Warning: Graphic sex, spanking, public fondling, more spanking, the ménage of the century, even more spanking, cranky ex-lovers, bondage and the misuse of both a piano and pool table.

Look for these titles by *Dominique Adair*

Now Available:

Jane Porter Series
Seducing Jane Porter (Book 1)
Educating Jane Porter (Book 2)
Reinventing Jane Porter (Book 3)

Writing as J.C. Wilder

Thief of Hearts
Winter's Daughter

Shadow Dweller
Tempt Not the Cat (Book 1)
Reckoning (Book 2)

Print Anthology
In the Gloaming

J.C. Wilder with Rosemary Laurey
Paradox I (Print Title - Sacrifice)
Paradox II (Print Title - Deep Waters)
Paradox III (Print Title - Stone Hearts)

Beauty Emerges

Dominique Adair

A Samhain Publishing, Ltd. publication.

Samhain Publishing, Ltd.
577 Mulberry Street, Suite 1520
Macon, GA 31201
www.samhainpublishing.com

Beauty Emerges
Print ISBN: 978-1-60504-542-9

Editing by Bethany Morgan
Cover by Anne Cain

Seducing Jane Porter, ISBN 978-1-60504-268-8
First Samhain Publishing, Ltd. electronic publication: December 2008
Educating Jane Porter, ISBN 978-1-60504-479-8
First Samhain Publishing, Ltd. electronic publication: March 2009
Reinventing Jane Porter, ISBN 978-1-60504-527-6
First Samhain Publishing, Ltd. electronic publication: May 2009
First Samhain Publishing, Ltd. print publication: January 2010

Seducing Jane Porter

Dedication

For Carol—girl, it's time to turn up the heat!

Chapter One

Being a sexual submissive was similar to Double Dutch jump roping, once you learned to navigate ropes, you never forgot the rush.

Both nervous and excited, Jane shook her head at her bad pun. Damn, she hadn't been this energized in a long time. She was as giddy as a child on Christmas morning.

Her palms were damp as she pulled on the narrow black strips of cloth that masqueraded as her panties. When the soft lace grazed her inner thighs, her sex tightened. It had been exactly one year since she'd participated in a scene and her body yearned to break her self-imposed drought. Twelve months without sex was more than any woman should have to endure.

She reached for the matching garter belt.

This time last year she'd been doing almost the exact same thing, getting ready to meet her master for dinner and hopefully more, much more.

When they'd met, Peter Ellington had literally swept her off her feet. She'd been dazzled by his charisma and panty-dampening smile. He'd showered her with gifts, expensive dinners and mastered her with a firm hand. In short, he was everything a submissive would desire in a Dom.

Her lips twisted. As far as she was concerned, there was nothing more dangerous than being in love. In her case she'd been so blinded by the sheer romanticism of his actions that she neglected to realize he was a complete and utter bastard. He'd used her love to his advantage only to leave her with a broken heart and a perpetually bad taste in her mouth.

Men!

Before entering into a master/submissive relationship, the sub needed to know the potential partner was trustworthy. The last thing any sub wanted was to be bound and helpless only to learn that their master was a psycho. Being vulnerable was both a turn-on and a potentially dangerous situation, so complete trust was important.

After Peter's betrayal, would she ever be able to garner that same level of trust for anyone again?

Picking up a silk stocking, she slid her thumbs inside the band to gather the delicate fabric between her fingers.

Anticipation had been high that night as she'd prepared herself for Peter. For months he'd been hinting at making their union more permanent so when he'd setup the date, her imagination took flight. They spent three to four nights a week together and he'd practically moved into her apartment. The only situation that could be more permanent was marriage.

Easing the stocking onto her foot, Jane shook her head at her own folly. How wrong she'd been. Blind, foolish and in love, she'd missed all the signs.

He'd planned a wildly romantic evening. They'd gone to an exclusive restaurant where the chef had created a menu of fresh seafood and decadent chocolate desserts. Champagne flowed like water and she'd been delightfully tipsy by the time they were finished.

After dinner the limo picked them up at the restaurant, and they'd necked like teenagers in the back seat. Upon arriving at his apartment, he'd cracked open more champagne and they'd spent long hours of bondage play before tumbling into bed, utterly exhausted and thoroughly sated.

During those quiet moments curled around one another, she'd thought he'd pop the question. She'd laid in his arms wildly content and dreaming of their future together...until he announced he was already married.

Her lips quirked. It was amazing how two little words—"I'm married"—could rock someone's world to the very core. Rather than asking her to be his wife, a position already filled by the current Mrs. Ellington, he expressed his desire to set her up as his mistress. She'd have her own apartment in an exclusive area of Denver and all of her bills would be paid without question. The only requirement of this arrangement was for her to be available to him whenever he called.

Jane snorted as she secured her stocking with the garter belt. Like that would ever happen. She reached for the other stocking.

For a long time she'd repeatedly kicked herself for not realizing he was married. Then again there hadn't been a pattern to their dates. When they had seen each other it was usually for all-nighters, not just a few hours in the afternoon. He'd been very generous with his time and lavish gifts that there'd simply never been any inkling of a wife.

Peter was a powerful attorney to the rich and shameless; that automatically made him an accomplished liar. Most recently he'd managed to keep a young starlet out of prison after she'd been caught with both narcotics and liquor in her car. In reality it wasn't a stretch of the imagination that he'd managed to conceal his marriage and three children for the two years they'd been together.

Shaking her head, Jane tightened the clasps on her stockings.

The frustrating part was she wasn't a stupid woman by any means. She had a master's degree from Harvard for crying out loud. She was thirty-six years old and a world traveler. She'd lived in Europe for several years in her late twenties and she'd experienced more than her share of lying, cheating men and still Peter had slipped past her defenses. Her friend, Lily, had once said Peter had pussy power, the ability to draw women to him from across a crowded room.

Prior to hooking up with him, Jane had had another dry spell in which the sprint up the corporate ladder had consumed her every waking moment. An overabundance of hormones after a nearly two-year deficit was enough to dull any woman's bullshit detector.

Picking up her corset, she wrapped it around her back then began the tedious process of closing the myriad of tiny hooks.

The only good thing that had come from her relationship with Peter was he'd convinced her to leave the corporate world behind and go into business with her best friend. Wasn't it funny that she had that bastard to thank for helping her make the best move she'd ever made?

She bit her lip. Even a year later, their final moments together were still fresh in her mind as if it had happened only yesterday.

One year ago…

"What do you mean, you're married?"

"You know, marriage, rings, kids—"

"You have children?" Jane's body tensed and her hands fisted against his broad chest.

"Yes." A gleam of amusement entered his gaze. "Three."

Stunned, Jane looked away from his handsome face. A

sharp pain lanced her chest and she was sure her heart was breaking. He wasn't going to ask her to marry him as he was already married. And with kids!

When her gaze met his, he didn't look nearly as handsome as before.

"Let go of me." Her voice was low, urgent.

"Whatever you say, babe." He released her.

"I cannot believe you'd enter into a relationship with me when you have a w-w-wife and children waiting for you at home." Flinging off the sheets, Jane rose from the bed.

"So, what's the big deal? It's not like you socialize in the same circles."

"Big deal?" She found her panties and pulled them on with shaking hands. "It isn't a big deal, it's a huge deal. What the hell ever gave you the impression I would have sex with another woman's man?" Her dress lay near the door and she stalked over to grab it. "I'm not that kind of woman."

"Obviously you are, you're here." His dry tone tore across her nerves like a scythe. "You were hungry for it, starving in fact."

"Only when I thought you were single," she hissed.

"I don't believe that, babe. You were so hot that night you'd have fucked whoever found you first. Count yourself lucky that I hooked up with you rather than some seriously twisted individual."

"Of course you don't consider yourself to be even a little bit twisted." Her laugh was harsh.

"Of course not. I'm a healthy male who is at his physical and mental peak. It takes a strong man to handle a woman like you."

Just what the hell did that mean?

With the dress in her hand, Jane could do little more than stare at the man sprawled in the bed. Only a few minutes before she'd been ready to give him everything, heart, body and soul and now she was so sickened by the sight of him she couldn't get out of the room fast enough. She pulled the garment over her head then yanked it down.

"One of the many things I've enjoyed about you is your unusually high sex drive. I've never met a woman who craves sex as much as you do." The lazy smile vanished. "You're very lucky that I came along when I did or who knows what could've happened. A woman, with needs as strong as yours, you might've taken up with any man to come along. Any dick in a storm, eh, babe?"

Her breath left in a rush as if he'd physically punched her in the stomach.

"You delusional bastard," she whispered. "You never knew me at all did you?"

"What else did I need to know, babe?" He flung back the sheets and rose from the bed. "You have a body made for sex and you're hot for it all the time. You're what any man would want in a mistress, a lady in the living room and a whore in the bedroom."

"Keep dreaming as it will never happen." She grabbed her handbag. Searching for the rest of her clothing, she stuffed each piece into the bag. Her hands shook so hard she could barely accomplish her task.

"I'll never be any man's mistress," she snarled.

"Come on, sexy. It's so good between us," he crooned. "Your body responds like perfection now that you've been trained to obey me."

His careless words were like gravel digging into her skin. Oh yes, he'd trained her well all right. He'd also blinded her to seeing what a jerk he really was.

"There will be no more obeying from me, Mr. Ellington." She struggled to close the zipper on her bag. "You are a liar and a fraud—"

"I know you're upset, Jane. Let's sit down and talk about this—"

"Not on your life."

She turned toward the door when his hand closed on her arm.

"Jane—"

"I said no," she ground out. "Let go of me you evil, two-timing bastard."

"That's enough, Jane!"

He jerked her backward and she lost her grip on the bag. Peter released her and she fell, clipping the edge of the dresser with her head. Pain raced through her skull and something warm and wet ran down the right side of her face.

"I won't let you go, Jane." He hauled her up from the floor then threw her on the bed face down. "You gave yourself to me, you made a promise that—"

"A promise to a liar means nothing!"

She started to roll to the side when his big body landed on hers, smashing her into the mattress.

"You're mine, Jane."

"Not any more."

Her voice was muffled by the comforter and she began to struggle. Just the feel of his body against hers, his cock against her buttocks sent a chill down her spine.

"I only lied because I had to, don't you get it? My wife—she doesn't understand me—"

Inwardly, Jane groaned. That tired old line was uttered in dive bars every night of the week all around the world. While it might work with some it certainly wouldn't with her.

"—I was so hot and you were so fucking gorgeous in that tiny pink dress..."

As he spoke his grip loosened, allowing Jane to free her right arm. Wrenching it backward, her elbow connected hard with his face. Peter let out a bellow as he released her. Taking advantage of the momentary distraction, she wriggled out from under him. Jumping to her feet, her cheeks burned and her body shook. She was quite sure she'd never been as angry as she was now.

Peter lay on the bed with blood running from his nose. He was alternately howling and swearing at her in a nasally tone.

"I'm going to kill you, bitch!"

Her gaze locked with his and she stood her ground. Somehow it was difficult to be really frightened of a naked, bleeding man who was howling like a girl.

"You will never touch me again, Peter." Her words were firm. "I'm my own woman and I gave myself to you. Now that I know the truth I'm walking away from you the same way as I came, of my own accord."

"You'll be back, bitch. You won't last a week without my dick inside you..."

Present...

Shaking herself from the dark memory, Jane fingered the scar on her right temple. Luckily her hair hid most of the mark as she'd hate to be faced with proof of her poor judgment every time she looked in the mirror.

Bastard.

She dropped her hand. The fact he'd pulled one over on her stung her to the very core. But what hurt more than anything else was his statement that she'd have fucked anyone who came along. He'd truly believed her to be a whore.

Just because she had a high sex drive didn't mean she'd fuck any man in the room. If anything, it had made her more circumspect when it came to choosing a partner. She'd never been one to leap into a physical relationship and in her opinion, masturbation was a sensible alternative to take care of her body's needs. She wasn't about to disrespect herself just to achieve orgasm.

From her first serious kiss, Jane loved everything about men and sex. The sights, scents, tastes and sounds of making love thrilled her on a visceral level. Once she'd learned what her body was capable of, she'd been eager to explore her sensual side.

Peter hadn't been the first lover to use her sexuality against her.

In her early twenties she'd had a boyfriend who'd accused her of screwing around on him. In reality he was unable to keep up with her sexually. As with all of her prior relationships, in the beginning her high sex drive had turned them on...then usually wore them out.

She shook her head. Just what was it about a sexually mature woman that threatened most men? It truly made no sense to her. Wouldn't every man want a woman who understood how to give and receive pleasure?

From then on she'd learned to hide her unbridled sexuality from her lovers. Besides, with a vibrator she could achieve endless hours of arousal without being stuck in the wet spot.

But a sex toy couldn't bind her wrists or spank her eager bottom. That could only come from a lover, a master who knew what to do to tease her body into the highest state of arousal before ultimately allowing a mind-blowing release.

That was what she craved; the feeling of vulnerability, of being tamed and treasured. To become a much desired sexual being encouraged to explore her deepest, darkest sensual fantasies.

Heat coursed through her veins and her clit hardened. Her eyes drifted closed and she swallowed hard. She'd yet to find that someone, the man who would teach and encourage her to embrace the dark side of her sexuality. The master who could set her free.

Her eyes opened, arousal was thick on her tongue. Peter had been wrong, though. It had never entered her mind to go back to him, not once. She'd made it exactly twelve months, one year tonight, without having sex in any form, including masturbation.

Jane reached for a miniscule black skirt. She'd never screwed around on a lover and she wasn't about to begin now. Well, when she got back into a relationship that is.

If...

She bit her lip. Could she ever trust herself enough to share her heart and body with another man? Right at this moment it seemed doubtful.

Stepping in front of the mirror, Jane's sharp gaze moved over her reflection. Thanks to her love of the outdoors she was in pretty good shape. Firm legs, wide hips, trim waist and her breasts had yet to realize gravity was calling.

She'd arranged her long blonde hair in a tight roll on the back of her head. Her makeup was subtle, mascara on her blonde lashes, a swath of neutral eye shadow and dark red lipstick. She wasn't sure why she bothered with anything other than lipstick as no one was going to be able to see her face anyway.

Picking up the bejeweled half mask, Jane slid it into place then secured the narrow ribbons at the back of her head. Shadowed by the mask, her green eyes looked darker, more mysterious.

Even she had to admit, she looked good enough to eat.

After a quick spritz of ginger-scented perfume, she was ready to go. Tonight wasn't about trusting someone, it was dipping her toe into the bondage scene. What she was looking for was mind-blowing sex, not happily ever after.

Chapter Two

"The men won't be able to resist you." Lily Tyler, Jane's best friend and business partner, linked her arm through Jane's. "I have to say, celibacy really does suit you. Your skin has a lovely glow this evening."

Jane laughed. "If I have to remain celibate to be attractive then I'll take ugly any day."

"Amen, sister."

Jane eyed Lily's curvy figure encased in stretch black velvet with emerald green crystals sprinkled across the bodice. A half mask of black lace shadowed her friend's lovely face.

"Have you looked in the mirror lately? You're far sexier than I."

"Well, that is true." Lily's laugh was incredibly loud. It reminded Jane of a blaring truck horn. "The men won't be able to resist us, and the ladies will hate us on sight."

"Isn't that the general plan?" Jane steered her friend down the steps toward the ballroom. "This is the first time I've been invited to Dirk's for an event as swish as this."

"Well if you'd make an effort to get out more, this wouldn't be the case..."

"I—"

"...though I know, you've been hiding out," Lily continued

without drawing breath. "That bastard was so not worth a year of celibacy."

"Well, it wasn't *for* him—"

"I know, but—"

"Well, aren't you just a know-it-all?"

"Stop being crabby, Jane." Lily gave her arm a firm squeeze. "I'm just looking out for your best interests."

"Then quick pecking at me like a nosy old biddy," Jane grumbled under breath.

"The important thing is that Dirk and Kitten are positively thrilled you're here for the weekend—"

"I haven't agreed to stay the entire weekend."

"You'll stay." Lily's smile was wide. "This weekend will give us a chance to expand our business in a big way. If the next two days come off without a hitch, our phones will be ringing off the hook. Everyone will want *the* party planners who pulled off this affair."

"You arranged this event, not I."

"But you held my hand when the string quartet cancelled at the last minute and I thought for sure I'd never be able to replace them."

"That's true..."

"Besides, it doesn't matter who did the actual work. It was our company Dirk hired so we both take the credit." Lily flashed Jane a wicked grin. "There are a slew of events this weekend and the guest list is a who's who of Denver society and I see no reason why we can't cash in on that as well."

"And tonight's celebration is for his half-brother, correct?"

"Yes, ma'am, Antonio Villareal is Dirk's half brother and he turns twenty-nine tonight. Dirk wants to make sure his brother has a very good time this weekend."

"Considering how much this party is going to cost Dirk, I would say his brother will have a very good time."

"Well, that is what they pay us for, a one of a kind experience." Lily laughed again and Jane could only wince at the abrasive sound.

They were both pleased their event planning business, R.S.V.P., was on the receiving end of Dirk's generosity. The Prentices were known for throwing lavish parties and when they received a call from Dirk, Jane and Lily knew the payoff would be a tidy sum. Her partner just loved to joke about how Dirk had single-handedly paid for their new offices from the basement up.

"This is going to be an event not soon forgotten. Many of the guests have flown in from all parts of the globe just for this weekend," Lily said.

"Hopefully we'll pick up a few referrals from this." Jane hugged her friend's arm.

"A few? Pish posh, people will be clamoring to hire us for their next event. R.S.V.P. will become an overnight international sensation."

"Well, it's hardly been overnight—"

Lily ignored her and pressed on.

"Dirk's plans are just devilish. It makes me hot just thinking about it." Lily giggled and it was only a smidge less painful than her laugh. "Just think about it, an entire weekend where you can be as wicked, wanton and insatiable as you want to be. You can pick your man and use his hair like the reins of a horse. The best part is that you don't have to feel embarrassed as you'll never have to see him again."

"The masks certainly help."

"They add to the thrill of the hunt. Not being able to see

your partner's face adds to the mystery...the intrigue of the seduction."

A shiver of anticipation snaked through Jane's breasts. Her nipples hardened at the thought of breaking her self-imposed sexual hiatus. But she still had some time to go.

"Not before midnight," she whispered more to herself than Lily.

"Midnight it is."

The volume increased as they neared the ballroom. Other partygoers lingered in the hallway and Jane was shocked to see that in comparison, she was dressed as simply as a milkmaid. Hell, she looked downright virginal.

The must-have accessory for this event appeared to be skin...and nothing else.

"Ladies."

A tall, broad man in a tuxedo approached them. His imposing height coupled with his faint French accent gave his identity away.

Jean Jacques Bertrand was Dirk's business partner and Lily's current non-obsession obsession. From the moment they'd met, the chemistry between them was so strong even Jane couldn't help but notice. For some unfathomable reason, the stubborn twosome refused to acknowledge the powerful attraction and instead they spent most of their time insulting each other.

"Good evening, Jean Jacques." Jane smiled widely as he took her hand and brushed his mouth across her knuckles. "You look very handsome this evening."

"And you look *très fantastique, cher* Jane."

"Thank you."

His attention turned to Lily and Jane didn't miss the flash

of pain in his shadowed eyes. She'd seen that expression all too often when he thought Lily wasn't looking. Stubborn fools. They needed to hook up and save any other unsuspecting suitor from a miserable existence.

"Lily." Jean Jacques tipped his head in the other woman's direction.

"JJ, how's tricks?" Lily's voice was shrill.

His mouth tightened.

Oh, brother.

It took every shred of self-control Jane had to not reach over and pull her friend's hair. Lily knew how much it irritated Jean Jacques when she shortened his name, which was exactly why she did it. In her attempt to keep the man at arm's length, she was acting like a spoiled brat.

"Ladies, may I escort you inside?" he said.

"Thank you, Jean Jacques, that would be lovely, " Jane said.

"Fab, just fab," Lily's gaze scanned the crowd, intent upon not looking at either of them.

Jane rolled her eyes. Her partner was far more interested in not making eye contact with their escort than walking into the ballroom. Jane looked up at Jean Jacques and his gaze met hers. He winked and she smiled. Maybe, just maybe, her friend had met her match after all.

She glanced down at her watch.

Less than two hours to go.

Antonio Villareal lingered in the gallery overlooking the ballroom. Dirk, Kitten and their first-rate staff had transformed the elegant ballroom into a cozy, intimate space. The cold marble floors were covered with a variety of colorful rugs and comfortable couches and chairs were arranged in small groups. Huge pillows were scattered on the floor and the guests were all too willing to make use of them.

A string quartet played in one corner of the room while the bar on the other end bustled with activity. Across from the quartet a low stage had been set up. In the center was a large square frame with chains and leather straps hanging from each corner. Beside that was a long table covered with a red silk cloth shrouding whatever was lying underneath.

Servers moved through the crowd with trays of wine, champagne and a generous selection of *canapés*. The hostesses were clad in leather corsets with short skirts, stockings and impossibly high heels. The black, glittery half masks hid their faces and lent the room a sensual, playful air.

The waiters were dressed in black pants with a white collar and red bow tie around their necks. The female guests seemed to enjoy their muscular physiques as they took their time selecting something to nibble upon. No doubt they were plotting how to turn their servers into dessert.

In all honesty, Antonio knew only a handful of the attendees. His half-brother had invited mutual friends along with some influential contacts in Denver. Dirk was hoping to give his little brother a hand in setting up the Villareal wineries here in America. They both knew it would only take a few well-orchestrated conversations to jump-start the process.

Antonio smiled.

What Dirk failed to take into consideration was that his little brother was a man who created his own brand of luck. At twenty-two Antonio had amassed his first million and at twenty-nine was well on his way to making his first billion. While he appreciated Dirk's thoughtfulness, handholding wasn't something Antonio needed.

"See any good candidates?" Santos, his lifelong best friend, stepped through the curtains to join Antonio. "There are some very beautiful women here, eh, *amigo*?"

"*Si*," Antonio said.

"Giselle is downstairs, she is looking very well."

"I wasn't aware she was invited." Antonio frowned. Why would his brother have invited his ex-girlfriend?

"She's near the door."

Giselle was a famous runway model and even with a mask, it took only seconds for Antonio to pick her out. Clad in a cream velvet body suit, every inch of her man-made perfect body was showcased to its best advantage. Her dark hair was loose about her shoulders in an abundance of waves and curls. In one word, she was lovely.

But he was no longer interested.

She was a beautiful, intelligent woman that any number of men in the room would be more than pleased to call his. Antonio was no longer impressed with her as he'd come to know her personality all too well. She was far more interested in gaining access to his wallet than his heart.

Their breakup had been stormy, much as their two-year relationship had been. Once she realized he wasn't going to come back to her, she'd launched a campaign to seduce him. So far she'd failed in her quest and that only made her more tenacious. His hope was sooner or later she'd realize he was no longer interested in playing her games.

"I'm sure she'll have a good time," he said.

"She will." Santos chuckled. "Giselle is not a woman to be left alone for long."

Just then, Jean Jacques entered the ballroom with a woman on each arm. Antonio recognized the redhead as the party planner, Lily something or another. She was fun, chatty and curvaceous and both Dirk and Kitten adored her.

His gaze shifted to the woman on Jean Jacques' right and his eyes widened. He literally felt as if he'd stepped onto an express elevator going down. His stomach dropped and his head felt oddly light, almost dizzy.

She was quite tall, maybe six feet, and her pale blonde hair was scraped back into a torturous twist. A red and black half-mask covered most of her face but her smile was wide. Jean Jacques dipped his head toward hers and she laughed, showing a flash of white teeth between her full red lips.

His breathing quickened.

This woman had a lush figure—so unlike the stick-thin body of Giselle. The blonde was curvaceous with real hips, thighs and breasts, the perfect hourglass figure. Antonio would bet his first million that a surgeon's scalpel had never touched this woman's flesh.

A red corset showed her ample breasts to their best advantage and her skin was creamy pale, the delicate coloring of a true blonde. A slim waist flared out to full hips and a plump, juicy ass. Taking this beauty from behind would be a pleasure with her soft buttocks slapping against his thighs as his dick plunged into her pussy.

He licked his lips.

Exquisite was the only word to describe her. She moved easily beside her escort, with a grace that was undeniable. With her easy smile and hot body, his cock was already standing at attention.

Considering she'd come to a bondage-themed party, her dress was modest. Her black skirt was longer than most though it showcased her long, shapely legs. The corset nipped in at the waist and just the sight of the tiny hooks down the front created an itch in his fingers. He'd bet her nipples were rosy and would taste like sweet wine.

At the tender age of fifteen, he'd lost his virginity to a lusty field worker at his father's vineyard. In the sun with the scents of crushed grapes and lavender, he'd worshipped her full curves and she'd made a man out of him. Ever since then his tastes had run to a larger, curvier physique with the exception of his most recent ex, Giselle. There was something about a plush female figure that turned him on. Just thinking of her, the baby soft skin and all those delicious curves to explore, sent all his blood rushing to his cock.

"There she is," Antonio said.

"Who?"

"The blonde on Jean Jacques' arm."

Santos made a noise of approval. "As always, you have excellent taste in women, my friend."

"I'm glad you approve."

"And will you share this one with your best friend?"

"We'll have to see how adventurous she is."

Antonio vividly remembered the first time he and Santos had shared a woman. They'd been at college here in America and Santos had picked up a beautiful Latino girl with long, dark hair and wicked hands. It had been she who'd convinced them to overcome their hesitation and join her in the bed. With that beautiful woman sandwiched between them, both men had experienced a deeper level of pleasure than ever before.

Over the years they'd shared many women though none would ever be considered a relationship. It was all in good fun and they treated their mutual women like queens both in bed and out.

The image of the blonde in his bed struck him with the

force of a hammer blow. Her lush body on his sheets, her silken cries as he ate at her pussy like a starving man...

His breathing increased.

Wet, hot, hungry for both of them...

His cock in her mouth, or her bare ass up in the air as Santos paddled her...

He gritted his teeth, glorying in the swift rush of lust that struck him. The sensation was thick like warm honey in his veins. His breath left in a rush and he swore. His zipper dug into his engorged cock with such force it was all he could do not to wince.

"Slow down, my friend, we don't even know her name."

Santos began to laugh when Antonio was forced to readjust his aching cock. His teeth gritted at the rush of arousal the innocent nudge created. Before the night was over, not only would they know her name, they'd know every inch of that beautiful body. They'd possess her mind, body and soul and she'd be ruined for any other man.

She would be theirs.

Chapter Three

While the hands of her watch inched toward midnight, Jane was feeling more than a little disappointed. She'd dutifully surfed the crowd and had yet to find any man who aroused anything other than amusement. This was not a good sign.

Everyone was friendly and more than willing to engage in a conversation or a laugh, but so far no one had managed to ignite a spark of sexual interest. There were a number of men who'd tried, but she was left cold in the face of their advances. Here she was ready to embrace her sensual side and there was no one to heed her call.

How was that for irony?

Jane scowled. She really was making an effort to enjoy herself. It was a diverse crowd, but her level of disinterest was high. With one man she'd found it difficult to discuss the latest box office smash while he wore a devil mask and his nipple rings jiggled with every word he spoke.

It was more than disheartening, it was damned near tragic. Here she was, all dressed up and no one to spank her.

Just when she feared the Jiggler was going to make a serious move for her, a woman in a skintight cream-colored cat suit arrived to distract him. More than grateful, Jane made her escape to snag a seat at a tiny table near the entrance to the ballroom. At least the view was good from here.

She stifled a yawn. Luckily for her she'd thought ahead and packed several erotic romance novels along with her much-neglected vibrator. If the clock struck midnight and she was still without an option, she would head back to her room alone. With every passing minute her solitary bed was looking better and better as her high heels were killing her feet.

With a gentle moan of relief, Jane eased her foot out of the left one, leaving the shoe to dangle off her toe. At this moment, taking off her shoes would be more satisfying than sex.

Now that was truly sad.

The blare of a trumpet took her attention away from her aching feet and almost jolted her off the stool. Swiveling, Dirk and Kitten entered the ballroom and everyone began to clap.

Dirk was a tall man with ruffled blond hair and broad shoulders. He was clad in black velvet from head to toe complete with a fluff of white lace at the throat. He reminded her of one of the Three Musketeers and he looked every inch a romance hero.

His wife Kitten walked by his side. Jane had no idea what her real name was, Katherine...Katrina....something like that. The bulge of the other woman's belly caught her attention and Jane's eyes widened. Kitten was pregnant, very pregnant. Even with the belly bulge, the woman still managed to look delicate and feminine beside her tall husband.

Her streaky golden hair was arranged in a complicated coil and she sported a dainty ivory mask. Her ripe figure was covered in sheer pink silk though she might as well have been nude. Her feet were bare and she moved with such a regal grace that Jane couldn't help but envy. Around Kitten's throat was a golden collar and Dirk carried a leash made of narrow golden links.

Both of them were smiling and calling out to friends as

Dirk escorted his wife to a plush couch near the stage. Once he was sure she was settled, Dirk kissed her cheek then took the stage. Raising his hand, he motioned for everyone to quiet down.

"Ladies and gentlemen." His voice was deep. "I'd like to thank all of you for joining us for this very special occasion. Tonight is my half-brother Antonio's twenty-ninth birthday."

A cheer rose from the crowd and the trumpet sounded again. A dark figure entered the ballroom just a few feet from where Jane sat. Her stomach clenched as he moved toward the stage.

He was quite tall like his brother, and he moved with an easy, catlike grace. Clad in black jeans and T-shirt, he was the only person wearing more clothing than she. Dark hair licked at his broad shoulders and he literally oozed testosterone. He had the physique of a man who worked hard for a living, from his wide shoulders and brawny arms down to a narrow waist and the tightest ass Jane ever had the pleasure of gazing upon.

All she could think of was sinking her fingers into the warm flesh of his buttocks. She'd bet her next paycheck that Antonio Villareal was an animal in bed. He possessed a barely leashed sexual energy that alerted every female of his presence.

She licked her lips. Maybe she hadn't waxed her legs for nothing after all.

Women crowded around him and he smiled and nodded at the ladies who reached for him though he stopped to speak to no one. Approaching the stage, he ignored the steps and leapt onto the platform.

A waiter walked onto the stage with a tray of champagne and the men each accepted a glass. Jane could barely tear her gaze away from Antonio. His plain black mask covered most of his face leaving only the lower half visible.

For Jane it was enough. He had a strong jaw and a quick smile that told her he used it frequently. A sense of humor was very sexy indeed.

"May I introduce my baby brother, Antonio?" Dirk tossed an arm around his neck. "The best damned brother a man could ever have."

Antonio's smile widened, "Better than you deserve, bro."

The liquid warmth of his voice trickled down Jane's spine as the crowd laughed. He had a slight accent, just enough to cause her to sit up straighter.

"A toast to my humble brother." Dirk raised his glass. "Happy birthday, Antonio."

Salut.

Jane raised her glass in a silent nod to the birthday boy.

Antonio took a sip of his champagne though he seemed preoccupied. His gaze moved restlessly around the crowd as if he were searching for someone—a woman perhaps?

"So now, my wife and I invite you to enjoy a special scene we'd like to share with you." Dirk was speaking again. "Please find a place to get comfortable as the fun is about to begin."

A scene? On stage?

Murmurs broke out in the crowd while Antonio and Dirk tossed back their glasses of champagne then left the stage. Within seconds Jane lost sight of the handsome birthday boy.

Her gaze darted to her watch. Only fifteen minutes to go.

People were taking their seats on the couches and pillows while Jane opted to stay put. Her gaze scanned the crowd and she caught sight of Lily standing off to one side with Jean Jacques. It didn't surprise her to see they were arguing again.

Even though her friend was almost a foot shorter than her companion, she didn't hesitate to get in his face. Well, his collar anyway. Her color was high as she poked her finger into his chest with abandon. His mouth was tight and Jane could tell he wasn't terribly pleased with being dressed down by a petite redheaded tyrant.

Without warning, Jean Jacques swept the mouthy woman off her feet and over his shoulder like she was a sack of laundry. He turned and Jane had to smother a laugh. Lily hung upside down smacking him on the ass and screeching like a loon as they exited the ballroom. Jane smirked.

So much for professionalism.

If he was a smart man, he'd find the nearest horizontal surface and he'd fuck her until she was too exhausted to bitch any more. They wanted each other and by denying it all they were doing was making those around them miserable.

A waiter approached with a tray of champagne and Jane took a glass. "Good night, Lily."

The golden liquid danced across her tongue and slid down her throat. In sheer bliss, her eyes slid closed. If she knew her friend, she'd either return to the ballroom bristling with indignation or Jane wouldn't see her for the rest of the night.

For Lily's sake, she hoped for the latter.

Being alone at the party didn't bother her, it wasn't like she didn't speak the language. Besides—she snagged a mini mushroom quiche from a passing waiter—the food was fabulous. And what was the next best thing to sex?

Food.

And then?

Taking off these feet-crippling shoes...

Kicking off the offending heels, Jane snagged a few more *canapés* before the lights dimmed. A buzz of excitement passed through the crowd. Two men dressed in black walked across the stage to move the restraint frame front and center. The chains dangling from each corner clanked against the metal frame and the sound sent a zing of arousal through her body.

Jane couldn't help but be fascinated. She'd never been to a party where a bondage scene had been acted out for the attendees. Of the few leather parties she'd attended, it wasn't unusual to see someone being spanked in a corner, but never on a stage in front of everyone.

Next they moved the silk draped table close to the frame before exiting the stage. The leather cuffs on the frame still swayed when a blond man mounted the steps. Every inch of his well-muscled body gleamed with oil and he was clad in black bike shorts. He was the only person not wearing a mask and considering he resembled a Grecian god, Jane was grateful for the unimpeded view.

In one hand he held a leash attached to a collar worn by a woman who walked at his heels. She walked with her gaze forward and head held high. She was tall and very curvy, what Lily would call a juicy figure. A red half mask shielded her face.

Clad in a white sheath, her long reddish blonde hair hung in thick curly ropes to the tips of her erect nipples. Jane's stomach tightened and her cunt gave a twinge.

The man led her to the frame before removing the leash. Taking her hands, he made quick work of binding her wrists with the leather cuffs. Dropping to his knees, he repeated the process with her ankles until she was fully bound with her arms and legs wide apart.

With the lighting as it was, her shift became sheer and her luscious curves were clearly illuminated. The sweet tuft of hair between her thighs was visible and Jane could swear she saw a damp spot on the sheath.

A male voice pronounced the woman to be "fucking

incredible".

The blond grasped the frame and released the lock. The frame rotated easily until the woman was facing away from the audience. Applying the lock, he secured the frame then reached for her.

Running his hand up the back of one leg, he raised the hem of the sheath to expose her plump buttocks.

Jane shuddered when he gave one ass cheek a firm squeeze. Moisture soaked the miniscule crotch of her thong panties. Never had she felt the desire to participate in a public scene such as this one though judging from her wet pussy, it was definitely a turn on for her. She licked her lips.

How did it feel to be on the stage in front of an audience and at this man's mercy? Her corset seemed to shrink as it became harder to draw breath.

The man ran his hands over his slave's plump buttocks, his tanned skin looked incredibly erotic against her pale flesh. He was speaking to her but Jane couldn't make out what he was saying. His hand continued its slow movement, pausing from time to time to cup a handful of flesh and give it a gentle squeeze.

The woman's hips began to move, pushing her plump backside against his hand as if to silently ask for more. A sharp crack rent the air and the room fell silent. The woman jerked away as if she'd experienced an electrical shock. A pale pink handprint appeared on her ass.

Jane's thighs tightened and she choked back a whimper. Her grip on the champagne flute tightened.

"You will not move until I give you permission, woman."

The deep voice sent tendrils of pleasure through Jane's body. Her pussy clenched again and she swallowed the champagne in an effort to relieve her suddenly dry throat.

The master moved away from the woman to a table covered by a red silk cloth. He yanked away the cloth and Jane's eyes widened when she saw what it had concealed. The table was covered with an array of sex toys, some of which she didn't recognize though she would enjoy making their intimate acquaintance.

He chose a leather paddle and Jane almost slid off her chair. A rush of liquid heat invaded her cunt and her nipples ached.

He ran his hand over her buttocks then replaced his hand with the paddle, gently rubbing it over her ass. Her hips jerked and he delivered a swift swat to tender flesh.

The tension level in the room ratcheted higher and one woman in the audience gave a lusty sigh.

The man began paddling his submissive, the sound of leather against flesh was heady. His slave tried to keep her body still but it was a losing battle. With every blow her receptive body twisted and strained against the cuffs holding her in place.

Her silken whimpers grew louder with each stroke and sweat broke out on Jane's upper lip. Tightening her thighs, though she wasn't sure if it was to bring on an orgasm or avoid it. She feared if she were to touch herself now it would be all over.

She glanced at her watch.

Damn, eight more minutes to go.

"You haven't obeyed your master." His voice rang out. "And for that you must be reprimanded."

He reached around the back of the frame and Jane heard the slide of metal. From the floor a wide black leather-covered table came up to the woman's waist. The top of the frame bent forward, forcing her to lean on the table to support her upper torso. This position forced her legs wider, leaving her dripping pussy visible to those who were watching.

"You are not to come until I give you permission, slave." He put his hand on the small of her back. "Do you understand?"

"Yes, master." Her voice came out high and thin with need.

He brought the paddle down hard on her wet pussy and Jane bit her lip to keep from crying out. The woman's shriek was long and loud causing a murmur to ripple through the audience. He continued paddling her, alternating between her ass and her wet pussy. Jane's body reverberated with each blow.

The woman strained against the cuffs, trying to lean forward to open her legs as far as possible. Her plump backside was angled toward him, eager for the punishment her master dealt.

Jane's arousal spiraled tighter. Her panties were soaked and her corset was at least two sizes smaller than when she'd put it on. Desperate for something to hold onto, she relinquished her flute then gripped the edge of the table, her knuckles white with exertion.

The slave's flesh had turned a glowing pink. Standing on her tiptoes, her weight was fully supported by the frame. She thrashed against her restraints, sobbing with her need for release.

Jane could sympathize with her plight. Shifting in her seat, she leaned forward to place more pressure on her clit.

The master continued the sensual torture and the woman's cries grew louder. The audience began to cheer them on; the voices growing more plentiful with each blow. Jane saw more than a few spectators were putting on their own little shows.

One woman, not ten feet away, had a man between her thighs eating pussy while two more laved her breasts with their eager mouths. They were oblivious to anyone else even being in the room.

A whimper broke from Jane's lips.

More than anything she wanted to be the woman on the stage. She longed to know how it felt to be mastered in front of a crowd, her arousal and submission on display.

Her heartbeat increased. She wasn't sure if she were more shocked or excited by what was happening on stage, all she knew was she was hot for the experience. The idea of being bare before a crowd of people while a talented master played her body like a musical instrument was enough to put her on the edge of a monster release.

The masked man dropped the paddle and began spanking her with the flat of his hand. The woman's cries of arousal turned to animal-like howls of pleasure.

Jane's breathing grew short and she shifted her hips to arrange even more pressure on her pussy. Her skirt eased up to flash an inch of her thighs over her stockings. Her level of arousal was both shocking and gratifying at the same time. She was only a hair's breath from climax and she hadn't even touched herself.

"You're ready to come, aren't you?"

Chapter Four

The sound of a Spanish accented voice in her ear caused Jane to jump. She turned to see who spoke only to have the stranger prevent her from moving. His hands, large and hot, landed on her shoulders. His warm breath caressed the nape of her neck and her nipples beaded painfully.

"No," she lied.

His firm tone coupled with the Spanish accent spawned goose bumps over her sensitized flesh. His voice reminded her of warm chocolate and rumpled sheets. Dare she hope this was the birthday boy?

"Watch her." His mouth brushed her earlobe and she shuddered. "Are you picturing yourself up on the stage? Can you imagine what she must be feeling right now?"

"Yes." Jane's body trembled. "I can."

"She is quite aroused, no?"

Her tongue refused to cooperate so she settled for nodding her head in agreement. On stage, the man had turned the frame so the woman was facing the audience. The frame had been adjusted and she was upright. Her master was working a bright purple flogger over her breasts.

"See how deft her master is? Gentle, delicate blows to follow the harder ones?"

His lips brushed her shoulder and she shuddered.

"He soothes her aroused skin with his hand, careful to not strike her twice in the same place."

His fingers tightened on her shoulders and his thumbs began rubbing the base of her neck. Her breath caught and the stiff corset pressed against her erect nipples.

"It is easy to see he cares for her pleasure more than his own."

"He's a considerate master," she whispered.

"That he is. Gabriel loves her very much." His warm fingers traced a blazing path up the back of her neck. "Are you new to the scene?"

Jane shook her head.

"You're a submissive." He spoke as if he already knew the answer.

"Yes."

"Excellent." Pleasure laced his deep voice. "Do you want to take her place on the stage? Would it pleasure you to have an audience while your master played your body like the sweetest guitar?"

"Yes." Jane squirmed in her chair. If she pressed her thighs any tighter she was afraid they'd fuse together.

"Imagine how aroused she is—" his voice dropped lower, "—her sweet cream is running down the inside of her legs. With each touch her body strains for release but her master won't allow it. Her pleasure is his responsibility, his gift to her.

"See how he gauges her response? He knows when to back off and prolong her pleasure. Their dance—it can last for hours."

Jane whimpered.

"Her heart beats wildly and her breathing grows short.

She's given herself to him totally, trusting him to take care of her needs. See how he worships her?"

Warm lips touched her shoulder and she shivered at the fleeting caress.

"She's close now."

The stranger's hands covered her shoulders, his long fingers coming to rest on the tops of her breasts. He eased her back to lean against his broad chest. The warmth of his body seeped into hers and his masculine scent surrounded her.

"With every stroke it becomes harder and harder for her to not reach orgasm, she's ascending the peak. See how she's pushing out her ass? She's begging for more, for something to fill her, his cock perhaps."

Jane tried to swallow her whimper, but it escaped anyway.

"Don't do that." Silken hair touched her shoulder. "Never stifle the sounds of your arousal they are beautiful as you are."

"They'll hear me," she hissed.

"Who cares? You want to be the woman on the stage where everyone will watch. Does it matter if a few see you here in the shadows?" His chuckle was deep, rough. "Gabriel and his slave hold the audience's attention in the palms of their hands. I could strip you bare and fuck you right here, and I doubt anyone would notice."

The raw image sent earthquakes of need through her body. She jerked and couldn't help but moan. Her tormentor's grip tightened.

"You're very responsive."

His voice was low and guttural signaling his arousal. Holding her closer, she felt a hard bulge against her hip. Running his finger along the lace edge of her corset, her breath caught and the burning in her pussy increased.

"I will taste you. I will dip my tongue into your pussy and lap up the sweetest of creams."

"Oh," she breathed.

"Then I will sink my cock into your beautiful cunt. Your flesh, so tight around mine, will weep with sheer joy as I fuck you." His teeth nipped her earlobe. "I want to spank your beautiful ass until your skin turns pink and you're howling with release."

Mother of God!

"I will bend you over my knee and..."

Jane's body shook, her need for orgasm was so acute it bordered on pain. She didn't know how much more of this she'd be able to take.

"...paddle you with my hands—"

"What time is it?" she gasped.

"What?"

"Is it midnight?"

"If I say it is, will you turn into a pumpkin?" Amusement laced his words.

"Q-q-quite possibly."

"One minute 'til midnight," he said.

A sob was ripped from her throat as one blunt finger worked its way into her corset. He caressed her nipple, and she jerked as if she'd been hit with a bolt of lightning.

"Spend the evening with me, beauty."

His tongue snaked out to caress the base of her neck. The touch sent a rush of heat through her body and she feared she'd burst into flames at any minute.

"Let me master you..."

His teeth grazed her shoulder.

"Taste you..."

A second finger plundered her corset to tease her other nipple. Her hips twisted, rocking forward, straining for release.

"I will seduce you..."

Her head dropped onto his shoulder, and her eyes closed.

"I will bind you to my bed. I wish to make you my most cherished slave—"

The earthy, vivid images created a series of shockwaves in her body. Arching back against him, her release was so close she could taste it. With the lightest of touches to her clit she'd explode into a million shining pieces in his arms.

"Very shortly they'll be serving a buffet on the terrace." His voice was thick and the accent heavier. "If you wish to become my submissive, wear this for me."

Something touched her shoulder and she opened her eyes to see a narrow red leather collar studded with crystals.

"By wearing this you will claim me as your master and I shall claim you, body and soul."

His lips touched her shoulder again, and she tilted her head to the side to give him better access.

"And if I don't?" she whispered.

"Then I shall have to try harder next time." His tone was amused.

"It's a very tempting offer, but I don't even know who you are."

Jane forced her heavy gaze to the stage just as the slave had achieved orgasm. She howled like a wild creature, much to the pleasure of the crowd. Jane's pussy wept, desperate for her own release, but it didn't appear to be on the immediate agenda.

"I've awakened the dragon inside of you and he will not

sleep easily," he whispered. "I am the only man who can tame it, tame you... I am the only man who can fulfill your darkest desires."

"I—" Words failed her.

"Say nothing now, beauty. It's the witching hour. Midnight."

When he released her, she felt dizzy. Her mind was crammed with the carnal images his words and touches had evoked. Gasping for breath, it took her several minutes to pull herself together after he'd left. Her gaze scanned the crowd looking for the man with the melted chocolate voice, but he was nowhere to be seen.

Disappointed, she sagged, exhausted yet her body still hummed with arousal. The intense hunger had retreated, but it was only on the back burner. It would take very little to rev up the heat again and she wasn't sure she'd survive the fury of her release.

Clutching the collar, she raised it to her lips.

Did she have the courage to wear it? The idea intrigued her to no end. She longed to be mastered and there was no danger of emotions getting tangled up as they'd never see each other after this weekend.

She was terrified, though she wasn't sure what scared her more, taking him up on his offer or turning him down.

Even though this was supposed to be his birthday party, Antonio wasn't in the mood to be a host. He was on a mission to ferret out the lovely blonde's name and to accomplish this he needed to find Lily.

Ducking out of the ballroom, he made a beeline toward the kitchen. Santos had seen them headed in this direction before the scene commenced in the ballroom. As he approached a utility closet he heard raised voices, one of them with a distinct French accent.

Throwing open the door, he found Jean Jacques and Lily toe to toe in the closet. Their cheeks were flushed and both turned toward him.

"What?" they snapped at the same time.

Lily scowled at Antonio, her hands fisted, coming to rest on her hips. "Can't you see we're busy here?"

Antonio was surprised. On the few occasions he'd been around her she'd portrayed the image of sweetness and light. It would appear the woman had a temper to match her fiery hair.

"Please forgive me, Lily." He gave her a half bow. "I need to borrow your companion for a few moments."

Her expression morphed from pissed to quite pleased. She flashed him a wide smile. "He's all yours."

"Thank you, Lily."

"You will wait here," Jean Jacques growled at her.

"I don't think so—"

"I did not ask you to think. You will do as I say."

Lily's eyes widened but to Antonio's surprise, she didn't respond. Just what the devil was going on here? His gaze moved from Lily to Jean Jacques. He'd never seen his brother's business partner address a woman with anything other than total respect.

Jean Jacques sent her a dark look before stalking out of the room. Antonio followed him across the hall, and he noted the other man had left the door open to keep an eye on Lily. He was bemused to see Jean Jacques was unwilling to let the mouthy redhead out of his sight.

"How can I be of assistance?" Jean Jacques spoke.

"Earlier, you came into the ballroom with a blonde woman. What is her name?"

"Caught your eye, did she?" The other man's smile was knowing. "She is very beautiful."

"Her name?"

"Jane Porter, she is Lily's business partner." His smiled faded. "She's also a good woman. If you or Santos do anything to hurt her you will both answer to me."

"I can assure you, I've never mistreated a lady—"

"Giselle has been telling a different story."

"She has?" Antonio had a sinking feeling this wasn't going to be good.

"She's telling everyone who will listen about how badly you treated her."

"Consider the source." Antonio snorted. "The only time I treated her with anything less than courtesy was when she broke into my apartment and I found her naked in my bed. I grabbed her clothing and shoved her into a cab while she screamed her head off."

"She says you cheated on her."

Antonio laughed. "She's a gold-digging liar with a vivid imagination."

"So it would seem." Jean Jacques' gaze was direct. "I have to admit her story didn't sound anything like the man I know you to be."

"We've known each other too long for me to lie to you." Antonio shook his head, truly sorry for Giselle. "I expected nothing more from her. She is a dangerous woman and a cunning liar. Because I am Spanish and I have money, people automatically assume I am some Lothario—"

"The women do at least."

Both men laughed.

"Take care with Jane." The other man nodded toward the closet where Lily stood still glowering at both of them. "As you can see, I have my hands full with this one."

Antonio leaned in and spoke in a low voice. "It's just my opinion, but if you were a smart man, you'd keep her lovely mouth busy with something else."

Jean Jacques gave a conspiratorial smile. "Trust me, my friend, I have every intention of doing just that."

Antonio walked away with a huge grin. It just might be that the boisterous Lily had met her match.

Chapter Five

Lily was very angry with him.

She stood where he'd left her, impatience written across every inch of her delicious body. When she saw him walking toward her, she relaxed against the counter and began inspecting her flawless fingernails as if she didn't have a care in the world.

Antonio was right, it was past time to claim this woman and show her who wore the pants in their sexually charged relationship.

"Are you done with your manly duties?" Her tone was bored.

"For the moment."

"Good, because now it's time to straighten something out between us, bucko." She pushed off from the counter. Her slim hands fisted and she braced them on her hips. "You're not the boss of me. How dare you interrupt my conversation with that lovely man in the ballroom—"

Her voice dissolved into meaningless chatter to his ears as Jean Jacques fell headlong into her eyes. Deep and green, they were flecked with hints of soft brown. Long, thick lashes framed her lovely eyes and even though they were spitting darts at him, he wanted to lose himself in the warmth of her gaze.

Scarlet lips spat words at him but he didn't hear them. He was too engrossed in her baby soft skin and the intriguing little blush that crept across her cheeks. Reaching out, he caught a lock of bright red hair. Tonight she wore it long and sleek like a waterfall. It was her hair that had caught his attention the first time he'd seen her.

As she shouted at him, the pale globes of her breasts danced to match her agitation. His gaze moved over her curvy figure. Her skirt was so short it was little more than a belt. Her stocking-clad legs were shapely and the sight of her black stilettos literally sucked the saliva from his mouth.

Lily was stunningly beautiful.

It wasn't any wonder he'd lost his grip when he saw the Austrian duke eyeing his woman in the ballroom. The man almost had his face buried in her breasts and it was all Jean Jacques could do not to toss the little man across the ballroom.

Though, in her defense, Lily didn't know she was Jean Jacques', not yet at least. It was a situation he had every intention of correcting.

She poked him in the chest—hard.

"You're not even listening to me," she accused.

"When a man is confronted with such beauty, he cannot help but become distracted."

Her gaze narrowed. "Oh, bugger off." She moved to walk around him. "You're impossible."

Jean Jacques captured her by the shoulder and spun her around into his arms. It didn't surprise him that she fit against him so perfectly. He'd known from the moment they'd met they were made for one another. Now he just had to convince her.

"What do you think you're doing?" she spluttered.

"What I should've done a long time ago."

She started to protest and he made his move. His lips touched hers and she stiffened. She whimpered and his grip tightened. Lifting her off her feet, he propped her delicious ass on the edge of the counter.

His tongue licked at the tight seam of her mouth and she opened with a shiver. Her hands crept up to his chest to fist on his lapels. Sweeping his tongue over hers, her taste was intoxicating, more potent than the finest wine. His cock leapt to life when she nipped at his lower lip. A silky noise sounded from her throat and his pulse leapt in response.

She smelled of floral perfume and warm, aroused woman. For over a year she'd tormented him to the end of his very endurance and the victory of having her in his arms was sweet, very sweet indeed. He wanted to claw every scrap of clothing from her body and worship her from the top of her head to the very tips of her toes.

"I wanted to hit him," he murmured. "I wanted to break him in half for daring to touch you."

"He is very handsome." Her voice was raw with need. "Any woman would consider him a prize to be won."

His grip on her thighs tightened and he growled. "But not you," he snarled. "Never you."

Pulling her to the edge of the counter, he took her mouth in a kiss that was hard, almost punishing. Her arms came around him, her fingers locked in his hair. He winced when she tugged though he enjoyed the pain and pleasure combination.

"Someone may see us." Her hungry fingers tore at his tie.

"They'll be jealous," he panted, "that it is me inside you, fucking your sweet pussy. Touching your breasts..."

Shoving his hand up her skirt, he tore her stockings and the delicate crotch of her panties. He was wild with the need to touch her, to feel her arousal against his hand.

"What if someone walks in?"

"Isn't that part of the game? The allure of possibly being caught by a stranger as I fuck you?"

She moaned, her emerald eyes were dilated and her mouth was rosy from his kisses. Dipping his fingers into her cunt, he was pleased to feel she was already wet.

"Yes, I want someone to see us," she panted.

Her eager fingers managed to undo his belt then open the fly. His cock sprang into her ready hands and they both groaned when her fingers closed around him.

"That's what I want to hear."

"Really?" Lily leaned away, her cheeks were flushed. "You're an exhibitionist?"

"Among other things."

Her green eyes widened. "You surprise me, Jean Jacques. I would've never guessed that of you."

He nibbled on her lower lip while his finger began to slowly fuck her sweet pussy.

"We all have our secrets," he murmured. "Now, are you just going to stand there with my cock in your hand or would you like to make his acquaintance?"

A slow smile touched her lovely mouth, and she gently squeezed his cock. Her grip was firm and knowledgeable as she began moving her hand in slow, gentle strokes. The rush of lust to his crotch was dizzying, and when she licked her lips, he knew he was in serious lust.

"So, my big man was jealous of that Austrian boy?"

He didn't miss the tone of satisfaction in her voice. Her thumb caressed the sensitive head of his cock, and he was afraid he'd spill himself right then and there. Damn woman, she was going to think he was an untried schoolboy. His teeth gritted, and he threw back his head when she settled into an easy rhythm.

"I like that," she purred. "Knowing you don't want any other man touching me, kissing me."

With her other hand, she cupped his balls, giving them a dainty jiggle and a gentle squeeze. Her fingers were magic and he felt as if he'd fly apart. His breathing increased.

"I have to admit, I do wonder if Antonio is a good kisser. I mean, the man has a magnificent mouth—"

Rage warred with lust. How dare she hold his cock and allow another man's name to pass her lips. His chin came down and he pinned her with an affronted glare.

"You will speak of no other man than me," he commanded.

Her eyes narrowed and he knew she was pissed.

"You did not just say that to—"

Grabbing her by the hips, he picked her up. She gasped and reached for his neck to keep her balance. Swinging her around, they hit the wall with a thud, his cock nestled against her sweet pussy.

"Do you hear me?" he growled.

"Y-yes."

With a roar, he entered her with the clumsy grace of an animal in rut. Together they moaned as his cock descended into her lush cunt. She was liquid silk surrounding him, pulling him down into the carnal darkness. Her legs wrapped around his waist and she arched her back, pressing her pussy into him, her clit in direct contact with his raging cock.

"No man will touch you ever again, Lily." He growled as his hips began to thrust. "No man but me."

A long, hungry sigh was her response.

"You're mine, you will give yourself to me."

"Yes." Her voice was high and thin. "I'm yours, Jean Jacques."

Burying his face in her throat, his mind went blank of everything except the woman trapped between him and the wall. His cock slid in and out of her sweet cunt, and his breath hissed through his teeth. Her capitulation was enough to send him over the edge all too soon. His release tore through him in a tidal wave of heat, and a hoarse cry exploded from his mouth.

Beneath him she tightened, her body spasmed around his, drawing out his release. Her breathy cries mingled with his and his hips slowed.

The moment passed and Jean Jacques felt both elated and drained. He raised his head high enough so that their foreheads touched. Her eyes were closed, and she was breathing hard. Never had she looked more beautiful to him.

She might be the death of him, but at least he'd die a very happy man.

Chapter Six

Jane's hands trembled as she toyed with the studded collar. The chimes announcing the open buffet had come and gone and still she dithered in her room. Should she? Or shouldn't she?

Do it.

She licked her lips. Isn't this what she came here for? To find a man who was willing to explore the boundaries of her sexual dark side? Sexually, she was a starving woman.

Her stomach clenched as her restless fingers stroked the soft leather. It was lovely, fine red leather with crystal studs. Most of the ones she'd seen downstairs were plain leather in a variety of colors though she hadn't seen any with studs such as these.

Brushing her nail over one of the studs, she frowned. If she didn't know better, she'd swear the crystals were diamonds. Her nose wrinkled. What kind of person could afford a diamond collar?

I want this.

Jane couldn't deny she wanted to wear the collar. She wanted to walk downstairs and claim the birthday boy as her own. Using only his hands and voice in the most modest of ways, he'd managed to bring her right to the very edge of climax. Her lips quirked. She could only imagine what he could accomplish with his mouth or his cock.

She groaned and her fingers tightened on the collar until the studs bit into her palm.

"Oh, fuck it."

In the back of her mind she thought she heard laughter as she secured the collar around her throat. The leather was butter soft against her skin. Even though she'd never worn a collar, it felt oddly right, almost comforting.

Mustering her courage, Jane rose from the bed and walked into the bathroom. Fear wouldn't serve her well this weekend so it was time to let it go and follow the demands of her starving libido.

Making quick work of removing the pins from her hair, Jane brushed out the long golden strands. Casting a critical eye over her appearance, she replaced the mask. The other ladies sported much shorter garments than hers. Wasn't this weekend about fantasy? About pushing the envelope and embracing her sexual side?

Taking the skirt by the waistband, she turned it under several times until the hem reached mid-thigh. The corset had created an amazing amount of a cleavage for a woman who'd always considered herself shortchanged in that area. An added bonus was her artificially flat abs. Granted, a bit of excess flesh appeared around her waist but it was nicely camouflaged by the skirt.

Screw stomach crunches, she could live with wearing a corset for the rest of her life if it meant she could still have her cake and eat it too.

Grinning, she slathered on a fresh coat of lipstick then blew a kiss at her reflection. With her heart pounding, she exited the bedroom and headed for the party.

The scent of food made her stomach rumble. Inside the

ballroom the lights were up and people were eating and socializing. The tables were crowded and everyone seemed to be enjoying themselves. She was hungry, but Jane doubted her nerves would allow her to eat.

Walking through the room, her gaze scanned the crowd but there was no sign of Antonio. Large French doors stood open at the far side of the room and the party had spilled out onto the stone terrace.

White lights twinkled in the ornamental trees and candles on tiny tables added to the illusion of privacy and seduction. Dozens of people occupied the area, but she didn't see the man she sought. Disappointed, she started to leave when the hair on the back of her neck prickled.

Turning slowly, she spied him leaning against the stone railing. He was flanked by several women sporting clothing far more revealing than hers, not to mention they were younger than she by at least ten years.

Self-consciousness reared its ugly head and for a moment she wanted to walk away. Antonio could have the pick of any woman here why—?

It doesn't matter how perky their collective breasts are, he chose me.

Lifting her chin, she approached Antonio and her gaze locked with his. Liquid heat rolled across her skin. A dark gleam entered his shadowed eyes and a surge of triumph raced through her.

She'd made the right decision.

"Excuse me, ladies." She placed a hand on his arm though their gazes never shifted. "I need to steal your companion as we have business together this evening."

"And the next." His tone was amused.

"Well, we'll see about that." She smiled.

A woman dressed in a pink corset jostled Jane, breaking her eye contact with Antonio.

"Look here, blondie—"

"Ladies, it has been a distinct pleasure talking with you." Antonio pushed away from the rail. "I must leave you as Ms. Porter and I have a prior engagement so I will bid you good evening."

"Tony—"

"Thank you for keeping him, amused, while he waited." Jane slid her hand into his arm and flashed them a wide smile. "It's much appreciated."

Together, they walked away arm in arm.

"You're very cheeky." His hand covered hers.

"I'm a woman on a mission. By surrounding you they became collateral damage."

Tipping his head back, Antonio laughed heartily and Jane smiled.

"I was glad to see you walk in," he said. "I think they were plotting on how to grab me and secret me up to a bedroom."

"*Mmm,* I wouldn't be too worried if I were you." She gave his arm a gentle squeeze. "You strike me as man who can take care of himself."

"We've known each other such a short time and already you know me well."

"I see you've managed to ferret out my name," she said. "So much for the mask."

"When I see something I want, I let nothing stand in my way of learning what I need."

A shiver ran down her spine.

"Are you always this resourceful?"

"I'd like to think so." He smiled and her stomach clenched again. "Can I interest you in something to eat?"

"No, I don't think I could eat anything right now. I think I'd like to go straight for....dessert." Her voice cracked, and she mentally cursed. She could only hope he didn't notice she was shaking from head to toe.

"A woman after my own heart."

He escorted her from the ballroom to the grand staircase. With every stair her ability to make conversation diminished. By the time they reached the second floor, Jane was sure her tongue was permanently glued to the roof of her mouth.

"Nervous?" he asked.

Mute, she nodded.

"It's important for you to remember nothing will happen that you don't approve." His voice was deep and reassuring. "In every master and submissive relationship, it is the submissive who's in command."

He opened a door then stepped aside to allow her to enter. It was a large room with a towering four-poster bed on one side and a spacious fireplace on the other. A plush couch was situated before the fire and French doors led outside to a balcony.

"Can I interest you in a glass of wine?" he asked.

"That would be lovely."

"Red or white?"

"White, please." Jane drifted toward the fireplace. The scent of burning wood was soothing.

"This is from my father's vineyards." He opened a small refrigerator and pulled out a bottle. "I think you will find this to be more than satisfactory."

"How did your family get into the wine business?"

"My great grandfather started working at the winery when he was seven years old. Fifteen years later he married the owner's daughter and here we are today."

"Sounds like a romance novel." Jane sank onto the couch and kicked off her shoes. "Love among the vines."

"They were totally devoted to one another." Antonio offered her a glass. "My father said his grandfather never looked at another woman other than his wife."

"What a novel idea." Jane took the glass. "Thank you."

She took a sip and the crisp, white wine was exquisite. Tart yet mellow at the same time.

"Good?"

"This is lovely, thank you."

"I'll pass that along to my father." Antonio sat on the couch next to her. Even from inches away she could feel the heat emanating from his big body.

"What made you so cynical, Jane?"

Cynical? She took another sip of her wine. Was it cynical to learn from a painful lesson? Her track record with men wasn't exactly a shining example of true love and fidelity.

"I'm practical, there's a difference." She shrugged.

"Semantics." His gaze pierced hers. "So tell me, Jane Porter, how did you come to be here this weekend?"

Grateful he let the subject drop, she turned to faced him.

"My business partner did the party planning for the weekend. We own an event planning business and we plan parties, weddings, any sort of event someone might need assistance with."

"Have you been to one of Dirk's parties before this?"

"No."

"And did you know what you were getting into?"

Her mouth went dry when his tone dipped even lower. The setting was incredibly intimate and Jane was both terrified and turned on.

"Yes."

"Indeed." He smiled. "And to think I'd pegged you as being quite...innocent."

"I am thirty-six years old, Mr. Villareal, there are very few things of which I'm innocent."

"*Touché.*" His smile was lazy, intimate. "You're a very beautiful woman, Jane."

"Thank you." To her horror she felt her cheeks heat.

"Don't go all shy on me now." He chuckled. "You have a regal air about you. A real 'don't touch me' essence. I'll bet men flock to you."

"I wouldn't go that far." Her heart was pounding so hard she was afraid he'd hear it.

"You appear so cool with that blonde hair, but I detect a simmering fire beneath the surface. You are a woman of great passion and desire, are you not, Jane Porter?"

She loved how he said her full name as if it were only her first.

"I'm struck by an overpowering desire to kiss you."

Her breath caught and a warm cascade of arousal trickled through her body. All of her life she'd been told she was pretty, but in his eyes, for the first time ever, she felt beautiful.

"So what's stopping you?" Her voice came out in a husky whisper.

"My stepmother." A smile hovered over his firm lips.

Jane blinked.

"She was determined that I have good manners and she would scold me if she knew the thoughts running through my mind right now." He put his wineglass on the table behind the couch. "From the moment you entered the ballroom, all I could think about was how much I wanted to claim you as my own."

A strangled sound escaped her throat and she almost dropped her glass in her haste to touch him. Setting it on an end table, she reached for him.

"You're an impulsive woman." Antonio pulled her into his lap. "I like that."

"Not normally." Her laugh was nervous.

She placed her hands on his big chest and once again a rush of nerves stole her ability to speak. He was so big, much bigger than he appeared from the other end of the couch. His thighs were rock hard and the bulge of his erection against her hip was unmistakable. The spicy, faintly musky scent of his skin set her nerves to dancing and her head grew light. She bit her lower lip and his gaze dropped to her mouth.

"A submissive must be prepared to bend her will to that of her master's." His hand settled on her thigh.

"I'm not looking for happily ever after," she blurted.

His dark brow arched as he considered her words. Silently she cursed her wayward tongue.

"I see," he said. "Would you like me to be your master this evening?"

She nodded.

"And in the morning you will decide if you to be my submissive for the rest of the weekend?"

She nodded again.

"As you wish..."

His breath mingled with hers and the first touch of his lips was as soft as butterfly wings. Lightly his tongue caressed the seam of her mouth silently asking for entrance. Her lips parted and her tongue slid across his. The taste of wine and man rocked her world. A silken moan broke free.

Sliding his arm around her shoulders, he pulled her close. The stiff corset prevented her from feeling him, but the warmth of his body against her exposed flesh was heady. If she'd been standing her knees would be shaking. Her arms crept around his neck.

Their kiss was a dance of seduction and she sensed Antonio was holding back. Was he afraid of scaring her or was he giving her a way out? Did she want an easy escape?

Hell, no. She wanted this man to fuck her until she couldn't see straight.

She nipped his lower lip and the response was immediate.

Antonio swung her around until her back was cushioned against his arm and the couch. His other hand slid under her skirt and along her thigh. When he broached the waist of her panties, her thighs automatically tightened.

"Relax, Jane," he spoke against her lips. "Nothing will happen that you don't want. Remember, this is your game."

She tipped her head back allowing him better access to her neck. With his teeth, he tugged on the collar then moved up to nip her throat. A bolt of arousal stabbed at her core and her nails dug into his shoulders.

"You like that." He nipped her earlobe.

"Yes."

"That little edge of pain with your pleasure." He kissed the curve of her shoulder. "It enhances your arousal and brings it sharply into focus. You are more aware of your need when you feel that touch of pain."

His accent was thicker now, undoubtedly a result of his arousal. That coupled with his hand moving up her thigh, left her breathless. Her need had taken over leaving her liquid, hot and aroused. The itch that had plagued her for a year was demanding to be appeased.

"Please..."

"In good time, Jane." His broad hand moved to the inside of her knee. "Anticipation makes the pleasure much more intense. Your release, when you receive it, will be the sweetest reward."

She moaned when his hand slid up her thigh to caress the damp material covering her pussy. Her thighs tightened, eliciting a soft hiss from Antonio.

Deft fingers pushed aside the thong and she whimpered when he gently tugged the soft hairs covering her pussy. Her arms tightened around his shoulders and she pressed close, silently begging him to touch her. Sliding into her slick cunt, he bypassed her clit to stroke the sensitized labia.

"You're killing me," she hissed. Spreading her thighs, she granted him better access to her needy flesh.

"If so, then you shall die a very happy woman." He chuckled.

When his finger brushed her clitoris, Jane jerked. Antonio removed his hand to reach up and pull off her mask. She blinked, feeling suddenly naked beneath his gaze.

"Exquisite," he breathed.

His fingers caressed her cheek then moved down her jaw. When his thumb caressed the curve of her mouth, her tongue darted out. The taste of her own arousal was shocking and thrilling at the same time. His dark gaze pinned hers and she longed to sink into the twin whirlpools of heat and need in their depths.

"Antonio," she hissed.

To her dismay, rather than touch her, he eased her from his lap onto the couch beside him.

"What are you doing?"

"I'm about to have dessert."

Dessert? He was going to eat *now*?

Sliding off the couch, he moved between her thighs. Taking her by the backs of the legs, he pulled her toward him, forcing her legs father apart.

Oh...*that* kind of dessert.

With a mask covering most of his face, there was something very naughty about letting a man go down on her when she wouldn't recognize him on the street.

Pushing aside her panties, he spread her thighs wide. His tongue was deft and with the first stroke she was shaking. His dark gaze glinted behind the mask and his fingers breached her molten pussy.

Jane's hips bucked when he inserted a thick finger into her cunt. She tightened around him and goose bumps erupted across her skin. Adding a second finger, he thrust in and out of her hungry pussy as his tongue continued its mesmerizing dance over her clit.

"Oh...oh...yes...yes!"

Her body arched and she pressed her clit hard against his tongue. With each stroke her need for release grew until she was screaming his name. Her nails dug into the couch, and her eyes slid closed. His hands gripped her hips to hold her in place as she rocked frantically against his mouth.

"Antonio!"

She reached for him, her fingers tangling in his dark hair.

When his teeth grazed her clit that was all it took. Her release was powerful, holding her body in its grip until every last drop of sensation was torn from her.

After a few moments, though it could've been hours for all she knew, the sensation began to ease and she sagged against the couch.

Damn. Why had she waited so long?

Chapter Seven

Antonio stood near the fireplace, his gaze fixed on Jane. She was still on the couch with her eyes closed and a sated smile on her lips. Her legs were splayed and the puffy lips of her hungry cunt glistened in the firelight.

She was more than he'd hoped for. Beautiful, intelligent and sexy and hungry, everything he could ever want in a woman. Beneath her cool exterior, Jane was liquid fire and the possibilities were endless.

With just a taste of her sweet pussy he'd almost melted into a puddle on the floor. Taking his time and getting to know her, her wants, desires, would be a pleasure he could not deny himself.

"Jane, are you awake?"

Her lashes parted and her hazy, sex-drugged gaze met his. Her lips were kiss-swollen and he was struck by the need to lick them.

"I think I'm awake." Her tone was thick, sexy. "If I'm not, don't wake me, this dream is too good to interrupt."

His lips twitched and he had to force himself not to laugh at her response. It was time to get serious.

"Come stand before me, Jane."

Moving slowly, she rose from the couch. In those sleepy,

sexy eyes, he saw the fire, banked for now, but it was there waiting to be released.

"Remove your skirt," he instructed.

For a split second she hesitated, her hands lingered at her waist before slipping it over her hips to pool at her feet. She stepped out of the skirt and kicked it to the side.

Clad in her corset, thong panties and garter belt, she was every man's fantasy. With her tumbled hair and swollen lips, she'd drive any saint to his knees.

Antonio was no saint.

"Remove your stockings."

She bit her plump lower lip then ducked her head to do his bidding. When she bent, he was afforded a mouth-watering glimpse of her breasts. Slowly she removed the stockings and sweat broke out on his forehead though he wasn't sure if it was her provocative disrobing or the fact he was standing so close to the fire.

"Put on your shoes."

Jane located her shoes and slipped into them.

Leaving her standing, Antonio walked to the couch and sat. Firelight danced over her plush curves. He was going to enjoy getting to know every inch of her body. Under his gaze, she shivered.

Good.

"Come to me, Jane." He was surprised to hear his voice roughen.

She moved to stand directly in front of him. Reaching out, Antonio pulled her down onto his lap. Her thighs bracketed his. Without hesitation he took the fragile thong and tore it from her body.

Her breath hissed between her teeth.

"You will not wear any form of undergarment unless I instruct you to do so. Do you understand?"

Her eyes went wide and she swallowed hard.

"Yes, Master."

"Remove your corset."

Jane reached for the row of tiny hooks.

"When we are together, you are no longer Jane Porter. Your name will be Beauty and you are my submissive. You will attend to my every need and command."

"Yes, master." Her head was down as she worked at the hooks with gratifying speed.

"If you remember these simple commands, I think this will be a mutually satisfying relationship."

Her pink tongue darted out to moisten her lips sending a rush of lust to his groin. When the last hook was undone, she removed the corset. Her breasts were large, the nipples dark and erect like berries. The only thing missing was a tasteful piercing, maybe a hoop of diamonds, from each tip.

Antonio leaned forward and touched his tongue to one pebbled tip. Her indrawn breath was sharp and she pressed into him. He pulled back, not wanting to relinquish his new toy, but it was time for her to understand that he made the rules, not her.

Sliding his hand up her thigh, his fingers slid into her slick cunt. Her hips bucked toward him and he shook his head.

"On my command only, Beauty."

His gaze speared hers. Their faces were only inches from one another though he made no attempt to kiss her. Centering his thumb over her clit, he began to stroke. Her cat eyes slitted and her jaw clenched as she forced herself to remain still.

Very good.

The scent of her arousal surrounded them and her cream ran down his fingers. Just watching her fight to remain still was a pleasure, but he had other plans for his new submissive. He removed his hand.

"Take off my pants."

Again she hesitated and he wondered at the cause. Her expression was oddly tense. Slowly she moved from his lap to sink to her knees between his legs.

Reaching for his jeans, she released the button then eased the zipper carefully over his erection. Lifting his hips, Jane slid down the pants and boxer briefs to his knees. Pausing to remove his boots, she pulled off the clothing before tossing them aside.

"I want you to suck me."

Silently she reached for him. Her slim fingers circled his erection and she dipped her head to take him into her mouth. He groaned when she covered the head with her soft tongue. Teasing the slit, her slim hand encircled the thick shaft and gave it a gentle squeeze that almost sent him jumping off the couch.

She took him deeper into her mouth, one sensitive inch at a time. The wet slide of her tongue coupled with the pressure of her hand around his shaft threatened to tear him apart. His hands fisted as she began to move over him, her mouth and fist moving in unison to stroke and tease every straining inch of his cock.

All too soon he began slowly pushing in and out, fucking her lovely mouth. His breathing grew labored and his movements frantic as his release neared.

"Stop!"

Jane sat back, perplexed. "But I thought—"

Lunging forward, his lips met hers stemming the flow of words. Taking her by the shoulders he guided her onto his lap. Their tongues tangled and his cock pressed against her wet pussy.

Before all of his brain cells were centered on his cock, he reached for the end table and grabbed a condom from the drawer. He broke the kiss, taking only seconds to sheath his erection with the thin latex barrier.

"Take me inside, Beauty."

Without hesitation she reached down to guide his cock into her sweet cunt. They both moaned as she sank onto his cock. The moment he was inside, Antonio needed no further urging. Gripping her hips he thrust upward, his breath hissing between his teeth. She was so tight, so wet he thought he'd lose his mind.

"Fuck me, master, hard."

Jane tossed her head back and she rode him easily. Her hips rose and fell in concert with his thrusts. Her grip tightened and he felt the tingle of oncoming release deep in his balls. It was too soon, but his ability to stop had eroded the moment she surrounded him.

Her nails dug into his flesh and her keening cries signaled her release. With a final thrust, Antonio gave in to the delicious sensation of her orgasm surrounding his cock. His body shook with the force of his ejaculation and his vision dimmed. Jane's movements had slowed though she still rode his body like a horse, stringing out his release to the *n*th degree.

When the storm passed, Antonio gathered her close and allowed his head to fall against her shoulder.

He'd chosen well.

Chapter Eight

Indian-style, Jane was curled up on the window seat wrapped in a bed throw. The terrace below was quiet as the revelers had headed for their beds...or their partner's bed. Outside the moon cast its cool blue glow over her.

What a difference a few hours made.

Her body ached in all the right places and her new master was sprawled on the bed asleep. Moonlight danced across his carved body, caressing it with the jealous touch of a scorned lover.

His face was turned away but she'd already memorized every handsome inch. Dark eyes framed with thick lashes, a straight nose and generous mouth, it was the face of a fallen angel.

Covering her mouth with her hand, she stifled her laughter. How many people could say they'd just experienced the most spectacular sex of their lives yet they had only seen their partner's face for a few scant moments in the darkness?

Gentlemen, drop your drawers and present your erections for the lady to inspect.

Her giddy thoughts brought forth an amusing image of a penis lineup. She couldn't help but laugh even though her mouth was still covered. The window was cool against her forehead and she struggled to stifle her merriment.

"I hope you're not laughing at me."

A rough, sleepy voice sounded from the bed followed by the slide of male flesh against the sheets. Their gazes caught and Jane felt as if every bit of oxygen had been ripped from her body.

Antonio lay facedown on the bed, gloriously nude. His long, dark hair was loose around his muscled shoulders and her heart jerked when he smiled at her.

"Are you?"

She cleared her throat. "No, I'm not laughing at you."

"Then what has amused you so?"

The image of the penis lineup flashed in her mind and she shook her head. "You'd never understand."

"I might surprise you."

"You already have."

"I'm glad to hear it."

His teeth flashed white against his copper skin and he rose from the bed. He was obviously comfortable in his own skin as he made no attempt to cover himself. There was an undeniable sexiness about a man who was unconcerned with his own nudity. He was secure in his body, confident about his standing in the world.

"Scoot over."

Jane moved to give him space to sit. He pulled her between his thighs then cuddled her to his chest. Male heat penetrated her flesh through the throw and she relaxed into his arms.

"We don't know each other very well." His voice was a pleasant rumble against her back.

"No, we don't."

"What do you say about continuing our friendship until the

end of weekend? I think we have chemistry that should be explored."

Hallelujah!

"I think that is an excellent idea."

His arms tightened. "What was that? I didn't hear you."

"I said yes, master."

He chuckled and placed a gentle kiss on her shoulder. Secure in the arms of her new lover, Jane leaned her head on his shoulder and closed her eyes. Slow leaden warmth invaded her limbs.

"I'd hoped you'd agree as I have much to teach you, Jane. The pleasure you experienced this evening was only the beginning of what your body is capable of."

"Goodness, I might not survive," she murmured.

"You will thrive, my pet. The largest organ of the human body is our flesh and I have every intention of seducing every last inch of yours."

"When can we begin?" Her words were slurred.

"In the morning. We will have breakfast and I want to introduce you to a good friend of mine. His name is Santos."

"*Mmm*...that sounds nice."

Are you on the edge of your seat? Are you dying to know what happens to our happy couples? Stay tuned for the next installment, Educating Jane Porter...

Educating Jane Porter

Dedication

Libby—it's time to expand your horizons...

Chapter One

"You have to tell me everything."

Lily's voice interrupted Jane as she was counting the crates of freshly washed glassware. The brunch was set to begin in less than an hour and her business partner had waited until now to show up? Jane wrote the number of crates on her checklist before she forgot it.

"A little late aren't you?" Jane kept her gaze focused on the list of items to be completed.

"I slept in."

I'll bet.

"I'm dying here. Tell me." Lily snatched the clipboard from Jane's hands. "How was it?"

"How was what?" Jane scowled at the redhead.

"You naughty girl. You're holding out on me."

"Give me my clipboard. Unlike you I have work to do."

Lily tucked the board behind her, and Jane rolled her eyes. Unless she wanted to engage in a childish shoving match, she'd have to wait until Lily decided to give it back.

"Lily—"

"The least you could do is look at me when you lie." Lily was grinning from ear to ear.

"I am looking at you," Jane snapped. "You can be quite tedious..."

Her attention was caught by a pale bruise on the other woman's throat. Lily had a love bite. Jane began to smile. It looked like her friend had a few stories to tell as well.

"You have a hickey."

"Son of a bitch."

Lily shoved the clipboard at Jane then pulled a silver compact from her pocket. She flipped it open.

"I told him to not leave any marks." She dabbed the puff over the faint spot on her throat. "I have to work this weekend, and I can't wander around with love bites all over me." She muttered the last bit under her breath.

"Mmm, I guess he didn't hear you." Jane bit her lip. It was all she could do to keep from laughing outright.

Lily shot her a dark look. "Well, you're looking pretty pleased with yourself for someone who has razor burn on your jaw."

"Drat."

Jane dropped the checklist and snatched the compact out of Lily's hand. There along her jaw was a faint pink line. Blood rushed to her cheeks. The burn combined with the sleepy, satisfied look in her eyes practically announced she'd had hanging-from-the-chandelier sex last night. It would be more subtle to take out a newspaper ad proclaiming the end of her self-imposed celibacy.

"It's not like you can hide anything from me, Jane." Lily sounded smug. "Not only am I your best friend and business partner, but your name has been on the lips of every envious woman here."

"Yeah, right."

Jane carefully covered the razor burn with the powder. She hadn't noticed the mark this morning, then again she'd been in a hurry to escape the bedroom before Antonio awoke. Having the most mind-blowing sex of her life in the dark with a complete stranger was one thing; it was another to face each other in broad daylight. She knew very little about him and he was seven years younger...

"Girl, everyone is talking about how you waltzed in here and took possession of the birthday boy last night." Lily made fake sniffing noises as she wiped away non-existent tears. "Mama is so proud of you."

"So am I." Jane shut the compact and tossed it at her friend. "I think I've got my groove back."

"Yes you do, my sister. And it's time to celebrate." Lily turned toward where the head of the serving team was setting up the bar. "Richard, can you bring me a bottle of champagne and two glasses?"

"Right away, Ms. Tyler."

Feeling like a child who'd skipped school, Jane allowed Lily to drag her outside onto the terrace. The wide space had already been setup for the coming meal.

Multi-colored pastel tablecloths gave the tables a floral garden feel. Each table boasted a round bowl of color-coordinated blooms along with silver trimmed china and an array of sparkling glassware. It was funky and elegant, exactly what Kitten had ordered.

Jane made a mental note to pass her thanks on to Richard and his staff.

Lily chose a table in the corner with a yellow cloth and a bowl of fresh daisies. Before they were seated, Richard appeared with the champagne and glasses on a silver serving tray.

"Ladies."

"Thank you, Richard." Jane took her seat. "The terrace looks lovely."

"Thank you, Ms. Porter." The man beamed. "I'll pass your words on to my staff." He poured them each a glass before leaving.

"Let's drink to your newfound sexual prowess." Lily hiked her glass. "It's been a long time coming."

"I'd rather drink to us." Jane raised her glass.

"And to a night of the most amazing sex ever." Lily's eyes gleamed with amusement.

"And may there be many, many more."

They touched glasses then Jane took a sip. The champagne was crisp, perfectly chilled and tasted just a little too good.

Even though it was barely nine in the morning, she couldn't help but feel hopelessly decadent. After last night, drinking champagne in the morning seemed tame in comparison. What next? Chocolate cake for breakfast?

Lily touched Jane's arm. "You have to tell me all."

"The only thing I have to do is assist with setting up the buffet." Jane teased.

"It can wait." Lily waved her hand. "After last night, no one will be down before ten at the earliest."

"Only if they were lucky."

"How did you manage to hook up with Antonio?" Lily's gaze drilled into hers. "I want all the details."

"Well, we ran into each other last night—"

"How? What did he say to you?" Lily snagged the bottle and topped off Jane's glass. "Did he come on to you first?"

Memories of last night's erotic show and Antonio's sexy voice in her ear washed over her. He'd definitely made the first move, and what a move it was... Her nipples hardened.

"He did, didn't he?" Lily's truck-horn laugh had Jane both wincing and blushing at the same time. "I knew it."

"You're such a liar."

"Am not. Ever since you accepted the invitation I've had a feeling about it. Jean Jacques mentioned Antonio's weakness for curvy blondes. I figured, after his last toy, he'd go for a grown-up for a change." She raised her glass in Jane's direction. "His taste is improving."

"What was he last girlfriend like?"

Jane wanted to bite her tongue even as the words came out. Hooking up with Antonio had been an aberration, a once-in-a-lifetime event that would read well in her future autobiography, after she made her first billion of course. She'd already decided on a title, *Born Again Virgin, the Jane Porter Story*.

Then again, after Antonio she might need to revise the title to *The Closet Hussy, the Death of Jane Porter's Love Life*. In her opinion, the chance of finding a man who was half the lover Antonio was, was pretty slim.

"Giselle is beautiful, sexy, a complete airhead and manipulating gold-digger to boot." Lily shrugged. "She's totally forgettable, which is why I'm so pleased he hooked up with you. I enjoy it when a good man realizes what's really important in a woman."

"Like what? A 401K?"

"You're so not funny."

"But how do you know he's a good man?" Jane asked. "You only met him a few weeks ago."

"It was several months ago and I listen to what people say. Dirk, Kitten, Jean Jacques, they all think a great deal of him.

Hell, even the household staff adores him." Lily refilled her glass. "With the exception of his ex-plaything, I've yet to hear anything negative."

"So he has the Lily Tyler seal of approval?"

"And you know how hard it is to accomplish that. Hell, I don't like anyone." Lily grinned. "He seems to be a genuinely good guy. A few weeks ago he and Kitten were discussing the funding of after-school centers here in Denver. The goal is to give children of working parents a place to go where they're safe and can use computers or play basketball. They want to hire us to plan the grand opening festivities."

Jane thought about the man she'd spent the night with. She could see him in the role of philanthropist. The way he'd wrapped his arms around her as they sat in the window indicated a gentle, caring side. She hadn't expected that from a one-night stand.

Well, a weekend stand.

"He's a really nice guy." Jane reached for her glass.

"But that's not what I want to hear." Lily eyes gleamed. "Is he a kitten or a tiger in bed?"

Jane began to laugh. Leave it to Lily to cut to the heart of the matter.

"Definitely the latter."

"I knew it!" Lily slapped her hand against the table. "He has that look that screams 'Wild Man'. You know, according to Mia, Dirk's housekeeper, Antonio's sexual exploits are...um...legendary."

"Really?" Jane lowered her voice and leaned forward even though no one else was on the terrace. She wanted to be sure no one overheard them gossiping. "How so?"

"I guess he and Giselle stayed here on numerous occasions

when they were together." Lily leaned toward Jane. "Mia said they had sex in practically every room of the house."

Jane's eyes widened. That was a lot of sex.

"They were like rabbits." Lily leaned back. "Well, he's young, and they say he's insatiable."

Yes, he is...

"And he can get multiple erections in a short period of time."

Oh yeah...

"Then there's his sexual wingman—"

"Wait a minute." Jane frowned. "A what?"

"A wingman. You know, someone who hangs with the leader and follows him—"

"I know what a wingman is." Jane interrupted. "But what is a sexual wingman?"

"They like to bed the same woman."

"They share their women?"

"No, Virgin Mary," Lily snorted. "They like to bed the same women at the same time. You know, a ménage?"

Jane swallowed hard. Last night Antonio had mentioned a friend, someone named Santos. He'd called him a good friend. Surely he wouldn't...

"His name?" Jane's voice was little more than a whisper. "What is his wingman's name?"

"I don't remember for sure but I think it was something Spanish." Oblivious to her friend's torment, Lily was busy inspecting her red nails. "Santino, Santiago or maybe it was Greek. Xanos maybe?"

"Santos?"

"That's it." Their gazes met and her friend's eyes narrowed.

"Did Antonio mention him?"

"Just briefly—"

"Girl… You'd better not be holding out on me." Lily reached for the champagne bottle. "I'll take away your key to the executive washroom."

"We don't have an—"

"Well, when we get one I'll have to give you the key then immediately take it away again."

"Will you focus, please?" Jane snapped. "So they take a woman, one woman, to bed? Together?"

"They've been doing it for years. One of Mia's friends was their playmate for a while, and now the woman will only have sex with two men at a time." Lily laughed. "I think they ruined her for any man flying solo."

Jane wasn't a complete dunce. She enjoyed reading ménage romances, but she'd never thought she'd meet someone who actually lived the lifestyle. There was something very naughty about just thinking of a ménage, naughty yet arousing at the same time.

"That's too bad, that they ruined her I mean." She downed the last of her champagne.

"Who are you kidding?" Lily's gaze took on a faraway look. "Can you imagine? Two men in your bed and all of the focus is on you and your pleasure. Yummy. Where do I sign up?"

After spending last night with Antonio, Jane could imagine it. Then again, she wasn't sure she'd survive two men at once. Antonio had tested her stamina last night, but two men!

A ripple of heat washed through her pussy.

"Peter did accuse me of being insatiable." Jane shifted in her chair.

"Asshole." Lily snapped back to attention. "He was too busy

looking at himself in the mirror to keep up with you."

Jane snickered. She wanted to enjoy her orgasmic hangover, and the last thing she wanted to do was to think of her ex. Besides, she could still smell her lover's scent on her flesh...

Pressing her thighs together to quiet the soft ache, she reached for the champagne.

"So, am I safe in assuming you and Jean Jacques have declared a truce?"

A telltale smile flashed across Lily's face for a split second before it vanished. She held out her glass for a refill.

"Not exactly."

"But you had sex with him?"

"Several times." She shrugged. "Having sex doesn't exactly mean we like one another."

"*Pffft.* Both of you have had the hots for each other from the moment you met," Jane said. "The problem is both of you are too damned stubborn to admit you need each other."

Lily's mouth twisted. "He's obnoxious..."

"Only when you get smart with him."

"Overbearing..."

"Protective and rightfully so."

"Boring..."

"You're such a bad liar." Jane laughed. "There is nothing boring about Jean Jacques, and you know it."

Lily glared at her.

"Besides, the man is as sexy as hell."

"Well—"

"You know, if you don't want him..."

"I will snatch you bald if you even look at him sideways,"

Lily snarled.

"His accent alone should be declared a lethal weapon," Jane said. "I swear, all he did was walk into the ballroom last night and women came out of nowhere to get close to him."

Lily sat upright as if someone had just pinched her ass. Her mouth went tight, and she did not look amused.

"Well, he is a free man."

"That he is. Jean Jacques is kind, good-looking and filthy rich. Any woman would consider him quite the catch."

"I suppose that's true."

Jane struggled to hide her amusement. Her friend was jealous as hell to hear other women had been eyeing her man. She claimed she wasn't really interested yet she didn't seem to like the thought of Jean Jacques with another woman. *Hypocrite.*

"You really should pay more attention, Lily. Last night this hot little blonde had her hand practically down his pants, and he wasn't exactly fighting her off."

Jane felt only a twinge as the lie passed her lips. She was damned tired of watching two friends sniping at each other trying to ignore their mutual attraction. The reality was both of them mooned over the other when they weren't around. It would be very sweet if it wasn't quite so sickening.

Okay, it was sweet, but she wasn't about to tell Lily that.

"Well, look at the time." Lily hopped her feet. "I'd forgotten, I'm needed elsewhere. Catch you later."

Before Jane could respond, her friend was off and running. With her Italian stiletto heels clicking on the tile, she vanished into the ballroom. Oh yes, Lily Tyler was pissed and Jane had the feeling that a very handsome Frenchman was the object of her ire.

She could only hope Jean Jacques didn't want to strangle her for lying. She lifted her glass in a silent apology. He might be in for it, but she was pretty sure the Frenchman could handle Lily. Besides, if she didn't throw them together, they were just foolish enough to miss out on the best thing that would ever happen to them.

Speaking of the best thing to ever happen...

An image of Antonio and her in bed flashed before her eyes. He was, in one word, delicious. With his fallen angel face and wicked hands, he'd rocked her world. Her nipples hardened. The way he'd moved, muscles bunching beneath her hands, his hips thrusting in a sensual dance that brought her to the edge over and over. She licked her lips as a damp heat engulfed her pussy.

But, Antonio and another man in her bed?

Me-YOW!

She drank deeply of the pale golden liquid. The thought of two men in her bed was a heady one. Several of her past boyfriends had felt she was insatiable. Peter certainly wasn't the first one to say it. Jane's lips twisted. What was it with men? They always said they wanted a woman with the libido of a man, but when they got one, they invariably fell short.

She bit her lip. It was possible that maybe, just maybe, she'd had the misfortune of hooking up with guys who couldn't go the distance. Maybe it had nothing to do with her after all?

Her body, aided by the champagne and a long night of sin, relaxed into the chair. She felt boneless and vaguely...needy. Jane slid her hand under the table to touch her pussy through her skirt.

Antonio certainly managed to keep up with her last night. But two, two men would be utterly sublime.

Two mouths...

Squeeze.

Four hands...

Rub.

Two cocks...

Suddenly aware of what she was doing, Jane yanked her hand away. Her gaze darted around the terrace, and she was relived to see she was alone. Her shoulders slumped.

Then again, she might be getting ahead of herself. Just because Antonio had mentioned Santos didn't mean he planned on inviting the other man into their bed. It was possible that he was just being friendly. Or, he might hope that Jane had a friend who might want to be hooked up with—

"Good morning, Beauty."

Antonio's accented voice flowed over her senses like warm melted chocolate. Startled, she jerked upright. A dark knit shirt accented every inch of his well-honed chest. His big hands, the same hands that had stroked every inch of her body, hung at his sides. Jeans cupped his body like a jealous lover accenting his height and his muscular legs.

Her gaze dropped to his crotch. The well-worn denim cupped the impressive swell of his equipment. She licked her lips. Would it be too forward if she were to demand that he strip down and fuck her on the table only minutes before brunch was to begin?

Their gazes met and the hunger deep in his eyes sent a rush of heat through her body. Daydreaming about him had served to turn her on but now, with him standing only inches away, she experienced a flash of hunger deep in the core of her body. Desire was too small of a word to describe how much she wanted him to touch her.

Jane cleared her throat.

"Good morning, Antonio. I trust you slept well?"

"For the most part." A smile curved his oh-so-talented mouth. "I was repeatedly wakened by a beautiful creature in my bed who was determined I attend to her needs every hour on the hour." His gaze dropped to her breasts. "She was quite persuasive."

"And was she kind enough to return the favor?"

"In abundance." His hand landed on the table in front of her. "And I cannot wait to have her in my bed again."

When their lips touched, flames ignited in her body. His tongue teased the seam of her mouth, and she opened for him. He tasted of mint toothpaste and hungry male.

She made a sound deep in her throat when he nipped her lower lip. Pulling away, his breath feathered her lips.

"I'm counting the minutes until I can suck that pussy of yours. Then I will kiss you from head to toe."

Jane was thankful she was sitting. If she'd been standing she was sure she'd be on the floor by now. Laying her hand over his, she squeezed his fingers.

"Mmm." She licked her lower lip. "You taste good enough to eat, Antonio."

His brow arched, and his gaze dropped to her mouth.

"Just the thought of my cock in your sweet mouth—"

"Ahem."

The sound of someone clearing his throat caught Jane by surprise. Antonio touched her on the chin then stepped out of the way.

Behind him stood a strange man who was watching them intently. He was tall, maybe an inch or so more than Antonio and his stance was relaxed. Where her lover was big and muscular, this man was whipcord lean like a long distance runner. His skin was slightly darker than Antonio's, and he had a vaguely Middle Eastern look to him. A diamond earring glinted in one ear.

Wearing jeans and a white button-down shirt, he looked totally relaxed. His dark brown eyes were deep, thoughtful, leaving her with the feeling that this man missed very little.

Whoever he was, this man was hot. Just standing there, he exuded confidence coupled with a restrained sensuality guaranteed to ignite any woman's fantasy. There was something about him, a European flair American men lacked.

"Beauty, I'd like to you meet someone," Antonio spoke. "This is my good friend, Santos."

Chapter Two

"How dare you!"

Jean Jacques drew the razor down his cheek. Lily, the woman who'd been screaming in his arms several hours before, was scowling at him from the doorway. Judging from her stormy expression, he was pretty sure she wasn't here to kiss him good morning.

He reached for a towel.

"Are you going to tell me what I dared to do? Or do I have to guess?" He wiped the towel over his face. "I couldn't have done anything to displease you as I've yet to leave my suite." He dropped the towel on the vanity. "I met this gorgeous redhead who wore me out last night so I was late to rise."

"Don't you dare sweet talk me," she snapped. "How dare you let some tramp fondle you before taking me to bed?"

"Fondle me?" He raked his hand through his damp hair. "What are you going on about?"

"I have it on good authority that last night, before you kidnapped me, you allowed another woman to stick her hands down your pants and play with your best friend."

His brow rose. A lot of things had happened last night, but he was pretty sure he'd remember a stranger putting her hand down his pants and playing with his cock. While he'd had a few glasses of champagne, his memory of last night's events remained crystal clear.

"Lily—"

"What kind of man are you? Hopping from one woman to another without remorse..."

Her words faded into meaningless jabber. Even though she was screaming at him, he couldn't help notice she'd never looked more beautiful. Her black business suit did little to hide her mouthwatering curves, and her sexy stiletto shoes were foreplay on their own.

His cock stirred. He was only sorry he'd never thought about making her jealous as green was definitely her color.

"You're a hypocrite, Ms. Tyler." He crossed his arms over his chest. He was crazy about her, but he would enjoy taking her down a peg or two. She was too arrogant for her own good. "Quite a few people saw you in the ballroom with the Duke in your cleavage."

"That's hardly the same."

Her spine was ramrod straight and it was a wonder she didn't snap it in half.

"How is it different? Another man, partaking of your..." his gaze dropped to her breasts. "...obvious charms and yet, you end up in my bed with my cock inside you."

Lily's cheeks were flushed, and her impressive bosom heaved with each breath. She was the kind of woman who wasn't familiar with the green monster nipping at her heels. He'd bet his left nut that being jealous was a new experience for her. Chances were she was more pissed at herself than the prospect of him fooling around with another woman.

"What do you have to say to that?"

Inside, Lily was seething. Jean Jacques had all but admitted he'd allowed another woman into his pants only hours before fucking her in the utility closet.

Jane was right, she'd been drawn to him from the moment they met, not that she'd ever admit it to him. Even though she'd fought the attraction, she hated feeling needy especially where a man was concerned, and now she felt used.

And betrayed.

Stunned by the realization, she stepped backward. No, betrayed was the wrong word. The only way she could feel betrayed was if she were in love with him—

"Cat got your tongue?"

Jean Jacques' deep, taunting voice broke through her panic. She stared at him, stunned to realize he'd moved closer while she'd dithered. The mixed scents of soap and warm male teased her nose. She scowled. He was too big, too masculine and he wasn't wearing nearly enough clothing in her opinion.

"Stop t-trying to in-intimidate me."

Her gaze dropped to the white towel around his trim waist. A thin line of dark hair disappeared beneath the towel, and there was a telltale bulge. A ripple of heat snaked down her spine.

Even knowing he'd been fooling around with another woman, she still wanted him. A sinking feeling exploded in her stomach. She'd known many women like this, willing to take whatever crumbs a man afforded her. They put up with bad behavior so they wouldn't be alone. Just the idea of lumping herself in with those women made her ill.

"You bastard," she muttered.

"*Chère*, there wasn't—"

His gentle tone lit a match to her anger. His lips were

moving, but she could no longer hear what he said. She would not let any man treat her badly and get away with it. She launched herself at Jean Jacques and hit him square in the chest. While he was easily twice her size, she had the advantage of surprise. Together they slammed into the wall.

"How dare you screw me after having some random stranger in your pants—"

"Didn't you hear one fucking word I said?"

"I don't want to hear your lies. You're just like every other man on the planet. An asshole!"

She swung at his head, and he caught her arm easily. Thwarted, she tried to drive her knee upward into his groin, but he sidestepped at the last moment.

"Damn it, Lily. Will you behave?"

"Not until I teach you a lesson—"

Jean Jacques cut her off when he grabbed her around the waist and swung her over his shoulder. Lily pounded on his back.

"What the hell do you think you're doing? Put me down, you manhandling bastard."

"Not until I teach you a lesson."

She heard the shower door open then he cranked on the water.

"I think you need to cool off, Ms. Tyler."

"Don't you dare put me in that shower. I'll kick your Frenchie ass."

He slapped her on the ass. She pinched him on the butt. The next thing she knew, he'd dumped her onto the marble floor of the shower. Ice-cold water hit her in the face.

"This-s-s is Versace!" she wailed. "You've ruined my favorite suit."

"Should've thought about that before you attacked me."

Blinking cold water out of her eyes, she stared up at the man who'd betrayed her trust. Tears stung her eyes.

"L-like you were in any r-real danger." Her teeth began to chatter. "You're twice my s-s-size."

"Your nails are longer."

Reaching for the faucet, Jean Jacques turned on the hot water. Lying on the shower floor with a half-naked, very pissed off man standing over her, Lily realized she was at a definite disadvantage.

Sitting up, she was grateful the water was warmer. Shaking the water from her eyes, she looked up his long, muscular body. Even though they'd spent the night together, she hadn't been afforded the chance to check him out.

Lily had always thought he was devastatingly handsome in a business suit, but now, clad only in a bath towel, looking at him was an entirely different experience.

His dark hair was damp and tousled. He had a strong face with brooding dark blue eyes. Broad shoulders melded into a muscular chest sprinkled with black hair. Her fingers itched to play with his flat nipples. His waist was narrow, and his legs were solid and covered with more dark hair.

Jean Jacques was incredibly sexy and more than a little pissed off.

"Feeling better?"

"Nope, still pissed."

He reached for the towel, and her gaze narrowed. He wouldn't dare...

The towel fell from his hips leaving his groin at eye level. Her breath caught. His semi-erect cock rose from a thicket of black hair. It was thick and dark, its vein pulsing as blood rushed to fill it. Slowly it lengthened to stand proudly from the nest of hair. A drop of pearly liquid seeped from the tiny slit in the head.

Even though she was soaked with warm water, she shivered. It was inexplicable. She was angry as hell at him and herself, yet she was ravenous for him, his cock. It was as if he'd never touched her before this moment.

The feeling that washed over her was new and terrifying.

"Are you pleased with what you see?"

Her gaze flicked to his face. He was smirking.

"It's nothing special." She shrugged. "If you've seen one, you've seen them a—"

Jean Jacques leaned down and grabbed the neckline of her ruined silk blouse. With a single yank the cloth gave way, baring her to the waist.

"Hey!"

Ignoring her, he stepped into the shower, pulling the door behind him. Lily tried to scramble away but he grabbed her by the knees. Yanking her forward, she fell backward. She'd never seen him so angry, so...determined.

Forcing her thighs open, he tore the away the crotch of her hose. She wore no panties and judging from the feral smile, he'd just realized it.

His big, thick fingers invaded her flesh. Parting her pussy lips, he entered her with two fingers. Her hips thrust upward. She was torn between wanting to smack his hands away or pull him down on top of her.

"Don't ever accuse me of fucking you after having had another woman," he muttered. "That's not the kind of man I am."

Withdrawing his hand, he shoved his hips between her

thighs. The head of his cock nudged her pussy, and he began stroking her clit with it. Need rose hot and thick in her throat.

Even though she was pissed as hell, she couldn't prevent the whimper that burst from her mouth. Anger had dissipated to be replaced with a powerful desire threatening to render her incapable of rational thought.

"Jean Jacques," she hissed. Her hips pumped upward to increase the pressure on her clit. "Please."

Removing his hand, he thrust into her. A keening wail broke from her mouth. The rush of sensation was heady, thick. Sliding her hand down to his ass, she gripped him tightly, silently urging him to thrust.

"Look at me, Lily."

Their gazes met, and she wasn't surprised to see he was still angry with her. She felt the same way about him.

"Hear me when I say I call the shots."

He rolled his hips, pressing hard against her sensitized clit. Her breath hissed through her teeth.

"For the past two years you've done nothing but make me crazy. We both know you're a little tease, and I've enjoyed the chase." He thrust again. "But now, right at this moment, I have you where I want you. On your back, begging me to fuck you."

Hatred and need burned through her nervous system. Digging her nails into his ass, she forced her hips up to meet his. Warm water rained down on them, shielding her tears from his gaze. Jean Jacques held her captive. His big body pressed her into the marble tile giving her no room to move. She was impaled and vulnerable to anything he wanted to do.

"Tell me, Lily. Tell me you want me."

"No." She thrashed her head on the tiles, need and pain warring in her heart. "I won't."

"You will." He thrust.

"No, please—"

It was as if she hadn't said anything. He continued thrusting, and his hips hammered hers. She arched, hungry for his touch, his mouth, his passion. The thrust of his cock in her weeping pussy was a delicious pain that stole her breath. Her heart cried for the man she'd spent the night with but she refused to let the words pass her lips.

"Submit to me, Lily, or I will fuck other women."

"I don't care who you fuck—"

His teeth bit into her throat eliciting a sharp cry from her. Need rode low and hard in her body.

"And you'll have to accept it, Lily. In fact, if you behave, I might even let you watch."

He was intent upon punishing her as much as she'd wanted to hurt him earlier when she'd attacked him.

"Damn you, Jean Jacques." She was sobbing. "Damn you to hell."

"You first," he muttered.

Her ankles locked around his waist allowing him to enter her more deeply than before. No longer could she feel the water on her skin. The man who moved over her had sunk into her body, her soul. They were one, bound by need, hatred and love all at the same time. She was sobbing in earnest, and her desire spiraled higher. Her need for release burned white hot in her belly.

"Until you give in to me, Lily, you will take what I decide to give you." His voice seared into her heart. "I will no longer dance to your tune for you're mine to command."

"No—"

Even as she spoke she knew it wasn't true. As he said, he

had her where he wanted her. She'd lost the battle before the war had ever begun.

His mouth touched her shoulder and before she could react, he bit her. Pain and pleasure rocketed through her body. Her orgasm exploded, and she screamed. Her cries echoed off the marble walls of the bathroom as wave after wave of sheer ecstasy burned through her. Her body shook with the ferocity of their coupling.

Jean Jacques thrust several more times. Stiffening, he roared out his release. Her hands slid up his back to rest on his shoulders. His big body jerked once more before he sank onto her, his head coming to rest on her shoulder. His breathing was harsh in her ear as shudders wracked his body.

Dear God, what had she just done?

It's him. It's *him.*

"I'm very pleased to meet you, Jane."

His voice was smooth, cultured like a fine brandy or the perfect cigar. When he assumed the chair next to her, his scent, a mixture of lime and healthy male, tickled her senses.

This man was hot, really hot. She'd never considered going to bed with another man so quickly after bedding Antonio, but—

When she became aware both men were giving her a curious look, she cleared her throat.

"Uh…it's lovely to meet you too."

Santos flashed her a smile that was both amused and pleased.

You're acting like a complete hick.

"So what brings you…uh…here, this weekend?" Inwardly she groaned. Of course he was here for Antonio's birthday. They were friends.

Santos's brown eyes twinkled. He took her hand and raised it to his lips.

"My friend told me the women were exquisite."

His lips touched her skin, igniting a quick flash of heat. When his tongue touched her knuckle she shivered.

Wow.

She didn't miss the glance the men shared. Her sex clenched.

"Isn't she as beautiful as I described?" Antonio slid into the chair directly opposite Santos. Between the two of them they'd effectively pinned her in the corner of the terrace.

"That she is."

"Blonde, elegant, confident." Antonio's hand slid under the table to settle on her left knee. "What more could a man ask for?"

"I don't know if I'm all that." Under the stare of both men, her cheeks heated.

"You are, and much more." Antonio's smile was intimate. He gave her knee a gentle squeeze and a warm ribbon of heat unfurled in her stomach.

"You're making her blush." Santos sounded amused.

"I enjoy making beautiful women blush."

Her lover's hand slid up the inside of her thigh pushing her skirt along with it. She sent a silent thank you to Kitten for requesting full-length tablecloths. Whatever he was up to, no one would be able to see under the table.

Antonio gently pressed his hand against the inside of her leg indicating his desire. Reaching for her glass, she opened her legs several inches.

"It appears you do it well," Santos spoke.

Another hand touched her right knee, and she started. Her gaze flew to Santos's face, but he wasn't looking at her. A waiter approached with them with three bowls on a tray.

"As you ordered, *Señor* Santos."

"Thank you, Ramon. The sun is warm, and this will be much appreciated."

Ramon placed the first bowl in front of Jane.

"I hope you like lime," Santos said. "I took the liberty of ordering for you."

"Why yes, thank you."

In unison, their hands slid further up the insides of her thighs, gently tugging them apart. Jane snatched her spoon as the waiter completed his service. He left with a slight bow.

Antonio's hand squeezed her upper thigh. Santos's hand moved upward and without thinking, she spread her legs. His pinky nudged her mound, and a rush of liquid filled her pussy.

"The flavor is exquisite." Antonio spooned a small amount of his peach gelato and offered it to Jane. "You'll find this to be a singular experience."

Though she wasn't entirely sure he was speaking to her, she obediently opened her mouth. The creamy substance landed on her tongue bringing with it the cool taste of peaches and cream.

Santos's fingers nudged her pussy.

"It is most pleasant."

Her gaze flew to his face. He was watching her with an odd little smile. His finger parted the slick lips of her pussy to delve inside. Electricity shot through her body when he touched her clit.

There is a stranger with his hand on your crotch!

Panic overtook her and from deep in her throat, Jane squealed. When she slammed her legs shut, she wasn't entirely sure if it was to keep him out or to hold him hostage.

"There is a shy quality to this dish." Antonio was speaking. "But if you savor the flavor, absorbing every nuance of its sweetness, it's well worth the effort."

Hell, they weren't talking about the gelato...

"Yes, I see your point," Santos murmured. Scooping up a small bite of raspberry gelato, he offered it to her.

"You will enjoy it, I promise you," he said.

Her stomach dropped. This was the moment. Santos wanted an invite into her bed. Her gaze darted to Antonio.

"I assure you, it is a flavor you must try." His smile deepened. "The experience will change your world."

Their hands on her thighs exerted enough pressure to alert her to their intentions. Need burned low, hot in her pussy. Her nipples ached with the need to be touched, sucked.

She wanted both of these men.

Jane opened her mouth to accept the bite. Cool raspberry delighted her tongue even as she relaxed her thighs. Spreading them wide, she gave them entry to her darkest desires.

"Pleasing, is it not?" Santos asked.

She couldn't even enjoy the bite because their hands were perched at the top of her inner thighs. At the first touch of her clit, Jane swallowed the bite.

At the second stroke, her hips thrust forward.

"It's lovely."

Her voice was shrill to her own ears. Quickly spooning a bite of her gelato, she stuffed it into her mouth.

"Soft, creamy. It's perfection." Santos stroked her clit.

"Sweeter than candy. I think we should indulge as much as possible before the party tonight," Antonio said. "It has been a while since I've indulged my love of sweet cream."

A finger prodded her vagina. Her breath caught, and she was penetrated. A second finger joined the first, stretching her. Delicate nerves leapt to life sending a gush of liquid need into her pussy. Her grip on the spoon tightened, and her knuckles turned white.

Judging by the angle, it was Antonio who was finger-fucking her under the table. Her nipples hardened, creating tiny points against her thin sweater. Fighting the urge to caress them, she took another bite of the gelato. The creamy dessert was melting under the warm sun, much like she was under the table.

From the right, a finger touched her clit. Her hips shot forward in a silent plea for more.

A bite of peach gelato appeared in front of her, and she licked it from the spoon. Antonio's greedy fingers in her pussy began to thrust while Santos stroked her clit. Antonio leaned toward her, and his lips brushed her cheek.

"I'm going to eat your pussy, Beauty."

A whimper slipped from her lips. Her gaze was focused on her dessert bowl, now filled with green cream.

"And then, after you come against my tongue, I'm going to put my cock into your hungry pussy and fuck you until you come again."

Explicit images crashed through her mind...her naked body, both men feasting on her flesh. Two cocks, thrusting, thrusting...

A sharp pinch on one nipple was all it took.

Antonio caught her chin and pulled her toward him. His

mouth took possession of hers stifling her cry. Their tongues mated as her orgasm whipped through her body. The whole situation was so carnal, so explosive. Jane was rocked to her very core.

The spasms eased, and so did the kiss. His mouth gentled, and his fingers in her pussy did the same. They removed their hands leaving her feeling empty, shattered. Antonio broke the kiss.

"You pleased me very much, Beauty."

She ducked her head, and he slid his arm around her waist then pulled her against his side. With the taste of Antonio thick on her tongue, she peeked up at Santos.

His gaze was direct, hot. Her eyes widened when he raised his left hand to his lips. His tongue slipped out to taste her cream, and his gaze turned fierce.

"That was quite enjoyable." Antonio was speaking to Santos. "Aren't you glad you took my advice and indulged this morning?"

"It was unforgettable."

Santos's gaze burned into her flesh, and she looked away. Just thinking about what they'd done under the table was enough to cause her heart to flutter. She'd just allowed two men, virtual strangers, to finger her under a table.

In public.

A rush of yearning moved through her body. Exhibitionism was a secret fantasy of hers, one she'd felt destined to remain unfulfilled. Her pussy clenched. Now, she wasn't quite so sure.

"I don't know about you, Antonio, but I'd like to taste more." Santos tossed his napkin on the table. "Shall we move our tasting upstairs?"

Chapter Three

When the door to Antonio's suite closed behind her, Jane feared her heart would burst through her chest. She was so nervous her knees were shaking.

"Don't be scared."

Antonio's lips brushed her ear seconds before his arms came around her. Grateful for the support, she leaned into him. Against her back he was strong and secure. His familiar scent worked wonders for the knots in her stomach.

"I'm not scared. Nervous, maybe." Her lips felt numb.

"I'd be more concerned if you weren't." He gave her a reassuring hug. "We spent last night in the bed over there."

Her gaze flew to furniture in question. It had been tidied up. The pillows were artfully arranged against the headboard and the dark burgundy duvet was perfectly smooth.

"Your experiences tell you there is nothing to fear from me, no?"

She wasn't worried about either man as much as she was concerned with what was about to happen to her. Giving up her body in the most intimate ways with not one, but two men, was daunting.

The French doors were wide open allowing copious amounts of sunlight to flood the room. Last night it had been dark, and Antonio hadn't been able to see her body. What if the extra weight around her belly grossed them out?

Even worse, what if this encounter did ruin her for other men? She didn't want to face a future lacking sexual fulfillment...

"Beauty."

Antonio's gentle voice jolted her back to the present.

"I trust you, Antonio."

"And you have nothing to fear from Santos. We've known each other since boyhood, and I'd trust him with my life."

"We only seek to pleasure you," Santos spoke. "You're a very beautiful woman, and it's only natural we'd want to possess you."

Possess.

A flutter started in her lower belly. Antonio's erection pressed into her buttocks, and her breath left in a rush.

"We're incapable of hurting any woman."

Santos moved to stand before her. His gaze slid over her face like a breath of warm air. He was just so damned sexy. A gush of cream washed through her cunt.

Reaching for the buttons, Santos removed his shirt. His movements were slow, casual. It was obvious he didn't want to scare her by moving too quickly. Judging from the liquid that trickled down the inside of her leg, he was succeeding.

Muscles rippled in his arm when he tossed the shirt over the back of the couch. His skin resembled pale caramel stretched over his rock hard muscles. Releasing the zipper on his jeans, he slid them down to reveal tight black boxer briefs and lean thighs. The sight of his barely contained erection sent quivers through her belly.

"I think our Beauty is enjoying the show, Santos."

Antonio's lips touched her neck and every hair on her body stood at attention.

Where Antonio was more animal with the long hair and bedroom eyes, Santos was urbane. With his black hair clipped close to his head and rock hard body, he exuded confidence and power. Every inch of him was a tough, sinewy masterpiece of male creation. Her fingers burned to stroke him.

The object of her desire reached for his drawers. The only sound she could hear was the thud of her heart. Soft cotton skimmed down his hips and thighs revealing a cock that made Michelangelo's David look like a babe.

He was quite long and thick like a tree trunk. Rising from a lush forest of dark hair, it stood proud and heavy with the need to rut. Coupled with Santos's darker skin, he had an exotic look that was undeniably arousing. What would his beautiful cock feel like as it thrust inside her pussy?

Her knees wobbled.

"Come, Beauty."

Antonio gently steered her toward the bed. She sat on the edge, and he joined her. His hand settled on her lower back, and Santos stood in front of her. A pearly drop formed at the small slit on the head.

She knew what he wanted without asking. Reaching for him, she wrapped her fingers around his cock, his skin scorching her palm. He was rigid and heavy, and she gave him a gentle, appreciative squeeze. Looking up at him through her lashes, she licked her lips in invitation.

His eyes darkened, and his nostrils flared. Leaning forward, her tongue snaked out to lick the pre-come from his cock eliciting a hiss of approval from Santos.

Beside her, Antonio murmured his encouragement while his hand began stroking her lower back.

Taking Santos's cock deeper into her mouth, she slid her tongue across the wide head then beneath to the sensitive underside. Slowly she began to suck him, her mouth and hand moving over his hard cock in slow, easy strokes.

Santos's fingers moved to her hair, fisting in the long strands. His grip was both tender and coaxing. Antonio tweaked her hardened nipple. She moaned around the cock in her mouth when Antonio gave the hardened tip a gentle tug.

Closing her eyes, she lost herself in the heady sensuality of the moment. With Antonio teasing her nipple and Santos's cock in her mouth, need burned white hot under her skin.

His taste was dark, earthy and forbidden. Curling her fingers around the base, she gave him a light squeeze. His hips lurched, pushing more of his cock into her mouth. His grip on her hair tightened, holding her in place as he began pushing in and out of her mouth.

Releasing her grip on his cock, she reached for his balls. Gently she stroked them with her fingertips.

"Slow down, Jane. Or this will end too soon," he hissed.

"Getting old, my friend?" Antonio chuckled. "You used to be able to go for hours."

"No," he muttered. "Her mouth is so damned sweet all I want to do is fuck it until I come."

Pleasure snaked through Jane.

"But I have other things I need to attend to first."

Santos pulled away, and Jane released him with a soft *pop*. Their gazes caught, and she was gratified to see his breathing was harsh.

"Look at me, Beauty." Antonio spoke.

Tearing her gaze from Santos, she turned. Arousal snaked through her pussy at the banked heat in his eyes.

"Santos and I are going to take you to bed." His thumb stroked the curve of her jaw. "We want to pleasure every inch of your gorgeous body. Your mouth, your hands, your breasts, your pussy, your tight little ass, all will be used to slake our lust."

Jane shivered at the sheer eroticism of his words. They were moving fast. Less than twelve hours ago she'd been a celibate business woman and now, two sexy, hungry men wanted to take her to bed. Not only would she have Antonio, but she'd have Santos to pleasure as well.

And to pleasure you...

Her clit began to throb. A gush of liquid washed through her pussy and her nipples ached.

Two men...

One woman...

One bed...

"Yes." Her voice was husky.

"Well, done." His smile was approving.

"Come, Jane, you're wearing too many clothes." Santos took her hand and pulled her to her feet.

Four hands seemed to be everywhere at once. In quick order her clothing was removed, and she stood naked between the two of them.

Surprisingly enough she felt calm about standing completely naked between two men. Knowing what they were about to do should've had her scared silly. Instead she was aroused and more concerned that if she didn't get fucked soon she would explode.

Antonio's mouth touched hers in a quick, hot kiss. Her hands fisted in his shirt, and she leaned into him. He easily supported her weight, and his hands came to rest on her back.

Another pair of hands landed on her hips. From behind Santos pressed into her, his erection nestled against her ass. Reaching between her and Antonio, he slid his fingers into her pussy. Her breath caught when he zeroed in on her clit.

"Oh!"

Antonio released her while Santos turned and sat on the bed pulling her with him. Jane was perched in his lap, his front to her back, as he slid an arm around her waist to anchor her in place.

Antonio's gaze was locked on her pussy and Santos's hand. He began removing his clothes while Santos slid his legs between hers forcing them further apart. She was totally exposed to the man who'd seduced her only hours before.

"Your pussy is exquisite." Antonio kicked off his shoes. "Have you ever removed all the hair?"

"Yes."

Jane's hips began thrusting against the fingers embedded in her pussy. With every article of clothing Antonio removed, her need ratcheted higher. Her fingers dug into Santos's arm.

"We'll have to see if we can get an aesthetician to come up and remove all your hair." He removed his jeans. "I'd like to watch."

"Mmm..."

Antonio came forward, his mouth coming down on hers. He ravaged her with a kiss so carnal, so earthy, she burned. Releasing her death-grip on Santos, she reached for Antonio. Her fingers tangled in his dark hair.

A rumble vibrated against her back. Santos's mouth touched the exposed curve of her throat. Her grip tightened in Antonio's hair, their tongues dueled in a selfish need for superiority. Santos continued his dizzying assault to her clit until she strained against his hand desperate for release.

Antonio broke the kiss. “I think we need to take this onto the bed.” Reaching for his boxers, he removed them. His cock leapt from the cotton confines as if to reach for her.

“I agree,” Santos rumbled.

Santos removed her hand and four eager hands urged her into the middle of the bed. She lay on her back looking up at the two men who were about to take possession of her, body and soul. Her breathing increased.

Antonio touched her knee. “I want to taste you.”

She needed no further urging. Spreading her legs wide, Antonio settled between her thighs. Bending her legs at the knee, he positioned her heels close to her ass. When he lowered his head, her hands fisted in the duvet. He parted the folds of her pussy and the cool air lapped at her overheated flesh.

Even though he’d barely touched her, she moaned.

Santos stretched out beside her. His hand came to rest on her right breast. His thumb caressed her nipple.

“You’re exquisite,” Santos murmured. “Perfect in every way.”

A strangled cry caught in her throat when Antonio’s tongue touched her clit. Stroking at the ultra-sensitive flesh, his fingers delved into her pussy, sliding in and out. Her hips began to move, following his strokes.

Santos’s mouth covered one nipple. His tongue laved the taut bud, then he started sucking. His other hand snaked across her chest to zero in on her other nipple.

“Oh, yes.”

Jane bucked and strained as they slowly drove her out of her mind. The delicious torment to her pussy halted, and the bed dipped when Antonio came closer. Santos relinquished her breasts, allowing his friend to take the lead.

Antonio moved over her. Reaching between them, he guided his cock to her pussy.

"Please. Please fuck me," Jane sobbed. Releasing her grip on the duvet, she reached for him.

His cock broached the sensitive entrance to her pussy. She moaned and thrust her hips upward. Impatience and arousal rode her hard. She wanted him inside her, and she didn't want to wait. Her eyes slid closed.

"Is this what you want, Beauty?" Rubbing his cock against her pussy, he pressed forward, parting her needy flesh. "My cock, inside you? Fucking you?"

He was torturing her. Her hands gripped his arms, the muscles were living marble. Antonio held himself over her, his cock mere centimeters from giving her what she wanted. Shivers danced along her skin.

"I want you inside me."

"That's my girl."

Pressing forward, his cock entered her, stretching the delicate nerves. She was sobbing by the time he covered her. Pushing her hips up, she took him deeper until she was stretched, filled to excess yet still she wanted more.

"Easy," Antonio breathed against her throat.

Wrapping her legs around his waist, she shivered when the root of his cock caressed her clit. It was hard to breathe, to think, with this man inside her. He thrust, and she struggled to regain control even as the rush of pleasure threatened to devour her.

Antonio slid his arms beneath her shoulders, angling his body low and tight against hers. He began to thrust, slowly and deeply. His body was hot and hard against hers.

Silky groans started in her throat as the tension spiraled higher. Her nipples ached, the hair on his chest sending jolts of sensation through them. With each thrust her groans increased in volume.

Teeth grazed her shoulder and her eyes flew open. Santos was close beside them, his gaze fixed on her face. Hunger burned in the depths of his dark brown eyes. A movement caught her attention. One big hand was curled around his cock, and he was roughly stroking himself.

The sight of those harsh jerks was enough to bring her to the edge. Her thighs tightened around Antonio's waist, and her release beckoned.

Without warning he unhooked her ankles and pulled away. Her pussy was empty and throbbing without him. Sobbing in protest, she struggled to reach for him but he moved too fast.

Santos sat up and grabbed her legs. Pulling her to the edge of the bed, he stood. Stepping between her legs, he caught her behind the knees and pulled her upward until her lower body was suspended over the mattress. He hooked her knees over his shoulders. When he entered her, she howled like a cat in heat.

Santos's movements were more forceful than Antonio's. His big hands dug into her hips holding her against him as he plunged into her weeping cunt. He moved with less finesse and far more urgency. With each thrust against her clit, Jane was mewling with the burning need to come.

Antonio settled himself beside her, his mouth covering her nipple. Sucking hard, his left hand slid toward her pussy. His fingers threaded through the soft hair, and he gave the strands a gentle tug. The spark of pain was too much.

"I can't..." she panted. "I just can't—"

"You can take me, Beauty."

Santos's voice broke. Any pretense of the urbane man was

gone leaving a hungry beast in its wake. His thrusts accelerated, and the headboard began to rattle. Antonio continued suckling her nipple, his wayward hand administering gentle tugs on her pubic hair.

Her body was relentless in its quest for release. Need rose hard, sucking the breath from her lungs. Her back arched, thrusting her cunt against Santos's cock. Release broke over her like a summer storm, her body buffeted by the waves. Ribbons of pleasure enveloped her body, and she lost all sense of time and place.

Lips touched hers as her body was lowered to the bed. Shivers raced over her skin, and she was unable to move on her own. Big hands gently lifted her, placing her in the center of the bed.

A warm male settled beside her and she recognized Antonio's scent. He pulled her against him, cuddling her to his chest. The bed dipped behind her, and Santos covered her from behind. His arm slid around her waist, and his hard cock nestled against her ass.

He didn't come?

Mumbling something, she reached back, and slid her hand along his lean hip. His skin was slick with sweat. His hand covered hers, and he held her palm against him. It was a tender gesture that allayed any remaining concerns she had about taking him into her bed.

Secure between the two men, Jane allowed sleep to overtake her.

Chapter Four

A mouth on each nipple woke Jane from her deep sleep. When she opened her eyes, she saw two dark heads close together over her chest. She threaded her fingers through their hair. She should have sought out a ménage situation years ago.

Utter relaxation enveloped her from head to toe. The sun had crept across the carpet telling her it was past noon, and they'd missed the buffet.

As if she could care about food with two sexy, hungry men in her bed.

They lay on each side of her, enveloping her in acres of warm male flesh. Twin erections lay against her hips while they feasted on her nipples. Someone's hand stroked her belly while the other covered her pussy. The blood in her veins had been replaced with liquid pleasure.

Santos lifted his head.

"We're pleased to see you're awake." Santos nuzzled her throat.

"Barely," her voice came out scratchy.

Antonio released her nipple. Raising his head, his gaze speared her. The sensual fire within his eyes was unmistakable. She turned. Lowering his mouth to hers, their lips met. Without hesitation she opened, and his tongue slid over hers.

Pleasure curled deep within her body as their mouths mated. Knowing Santos watched them deepened the pleasure. His breath was hot against her breast and it sent shivers down her spine. Antonio nipped her lip then released her.

"While you slept, we decided since we took such good care of you earlier, its time for you to return the favor." He kissed the corner of her mouth.

"Is that so?" She lightly drew her nails across their flesh. Her gaze met Santos's. "Do you agree?"

"I do indeed."

She leaned toward him, and his lips brushed hers. It was a faint touch that left her wanting more.

Beside her, Antonio rolled onto his back, and she sat up. His hands were tucked behind his head leaving every hard inch of his body open for her inspection. His thick cock lay against his lower stomach. Under her scrutiny, it twitched.

"Since you're both in agreement," Jane shifted to her knees, "then who am I to deny your wish?"

Sliding her leg across Antonio, she straddled his hips. Reaching between them, she guided his cock to her pussy. His gaze glittered with a dangerous heat. His hands came to rest on her hips. Her eyes slid closed as her body stretched to accommodate him. The sensation was heady and judging from the tension in his body, he was feeling as needy as she.

The bed shifted, and her eyes opened. Santos was propped against the pillows with his hand wrapped around his cock. Her gaze locked with his. When she moved upward on Antonio's cock, Santos's hand drifted down on his.

Leaning forward, she braced her hands on Antonio's chest. Her hips moved over him, his cock sliding in and out of her body in long smooth strokes. Santos echoed her movements on his cock yet his gaze never left her.

Liquid flooded her pussy. Antonio's cock created a sucking sound as she moved over him. The slap of flesh against flesh brought a feral smile to Santos's lips. Heat spread through her pussy, and her hips increased the pace.

Finally Santos broke her gaze to look down at his friend's cock moving in and out between her pussy lips. He licked his lips, and her nipples began to throb.

She'd already experienced two mind-blowing orgasms. What astounded her was, if anything, her hunger was stronger than when they'd come upstairs. It was almost as if taking these two men into her bed, into her body, had opened a part of herself that she hadn't dreamed even existed. A feral side of her sexual self was emerging.

Jane faded into the background, and Beauty emerged.

The pace of Santos's hand on his cock increased and a sheen broke out on his face. Triumph welled and power surged as her need for release increased. They might've seduced her but she had no doubt that at this moment, she held each of them in the palm of her hand.

"Stop." Antonio's hand tightened on her hips and broke her rhythm. Her gaze flew to his face.

"Up," he said.

Disappointed but curious to see what he had in mind, Jane did as he bid. Sliding his still-erect cock from her body, he rolled away to stand next to the bed. Both of them helped her to her feet, and Santos followed.

Antonio sat on the edge of the bed. Taking her by the hips, he guided her to him. She gripped his shoulders, using him for balance as she straddled his hips. Reaching between them, she guided his cock to her pussy. They both groaned as she sank onto him.

Santos's body pressed in from behind. His cock rested

against the crack of her butt. Jane quivered when she realized what they were up to. Santos wanted to fuck her in the ass.

Fear and desire crowded her throat. Alarm bells were going off in her head even as her arms slid around Antonio's shoulders. His hands gripped her waist forcing her to lean into him. Beneath her, he spread her legs wider. With her hips held in an arched position, she sank onto Antonio, lifting her ass toward Santos in silent invitation.

His hand palmed one ass cheek and gave it a firm squeeze. Her pussy tightened around Antonio's cock eliciting a hiss from him. She angled her hips higher putting her ass at the perfect angle for Santos to fuck her from behind.

She was surprised when Santos stepped away. Looking over her shoulder, she saw him grab a condom from the bedside table. After donning it, he removed a black tube from the drawer before he returned. His cock butted the seam of her ass, and she trembled.

"Easy, Beauty." Antonio's chest rumbled against her breasts. "Relax and we'll take care of you."

Jane lay her head on Antonio's shoulder. Behind her she heard the squelch of gel being squeezed from a tube. A hand spread her ass cheeks to expose her anus. Santos rubbed the cool, thick gel on the tight little mouth. When he inserted his finger, she gasped and thrust against Antonio.

"Easy, Beauty." Santos applied more gel using his finger to spread it inside of her anus. "I want to make sure you're ready."

An image of his cock sprang to mind along with a niggling worry. He was a big man, what if she couldn't take him?

She heard the tube hit the bedside table. Big hands spread her ass cheeks wide. The cool air hit the gel, and her anus tightened.

"I wish you could see what I do, Beauty. That tight little

mouth all rosy and shiny just waiting for me to fuck it."

Santos spoke under his breath. His skin seared hers, and his cock touched her. After positioning himself against the tight ring of muscle, he moved forward slowly. Her breath caught as waves of pleasurable pain washed through her. Her grip on Antonio's neck tightened.

The pressure increased until Jane felt the muscles release. With slow, deliberate movements, Santos's cock invaded her anus. He took his time giving her body the chance to adjust to his size. Just when she thought she couldn't take any more, he was buried inside her.

Jane clung tightly to Antonio. Sweat had broken out on her skin sealing his body to hers. With two sizeable cocks embedded in her body, she felt full—like never before. Her vision swam as she tried to assimilate the rush of sensations that assailed her, but the men gave her no time.

Careful to alternate their movements, they began to thrust. Fear vanished under the sensual assault. Antonio's hands slid upward to hold her close while Santos gripped her waist, helping her to move in response to Antonio's thrusts.

Time faded as the alternating thrusts ruthlessly forced her to a new level of arousal. Her body was trapped between the two men, a vessel of pleasure to be used according to their desires. She had no say in what they did. She was their captive.

"Oh, oh, oh!"

Her body tightened and urgency rode low and hard. Santos's thrusts in her ass grew jerky and uncoordinated. His hands tightened on her waist, and she arched as high as she could to take all of him inside. His cock stiffened, and his roar filled the room. Her body began to shake.

"That's it, Beauty. Take all of it." Antonio's voice seemed to be miles away. "All of us."

"Yes, yes, yes!"

Her body drew in on itself like a deep inhalation. His cock continued thrusting even as her body exploded around him. Light flashed before her eyes, and her nails dug into his shoulders. She was floating high above her body yet inexplicably tethered to each of them.

Antonio threw his head back, every muscle in his throat standing out in stark relief. His lips drew back and a feral snarl was torn from his throat. His hips thrust upward, his cock burrowing deeper into her pussy as hot jets of semen rushed into her body.

Spent, she allowed her head to fall forward to rest on his shoulder. They panted for breath, their bodies locked together like a piece of modern art. At that moment she wasn't sure where she ended and they began.

Santos moved first, easing himself from her body. He kissed her on the cheek then left them. Without his heat her back felt chilled.

"How are you feeling, Jane?" Antonio nuzzled her ear.

"Limp." Her voice came out as little more than a croak. She wasn't sure if she'd be able to move ever again.

He chuckled. "You're an amazing woman, Jane Porter."

She raised her head and their gazes met. He was smiling at her.

"You're pretty impressive yourself, *Señor* Villareal." Well aware he was still buried deep inside her, Jane wiggled her hips.

"Care to join me in the shower?"

"That sounds lovely."

It took a few moments to convince her body to move. Slowly she untangled her limbs from his. Now she could only hope her shaky legs would support her. Antonio's cock slid from her wet pussy setting off a curl of heat. She was amazed that after such a cataclysmic climax her body was able to feel anything, let alone arousal.

This was a new record for her.

Antonio took her hand, and together they walked to the bathroom. Just as they reached the door, Santos exited.

"The bed is all yours." Antonio grinned. "But don't get too comfortable as we'll be back."

"Marvelous." Santos's lips brushed her cheek.

Antonio started the water, and Jane stepped into the marble enclosure. Warm water poured from multiple jets in the ceiling and walls, and she sighed with happiness. The pulses of water felt good against her tired limbs.

Antonio joined her, with a cloth in one hand and soap in the other. Working the soap into the cloth, he drew it over her skin, carefully washing away the evidence of their tryst.

Charmed by his ministrations, Jane simply stood there as he bathed every inch of her body. His hands were sure, strong as they moved over her. In bed he'd proved himself to be a considerate lover, but this was a dimension of him she'd yet to experience.

Caretaker.

She hadn't known what to expect when she invited them to take her to bed. Hot sex? Yes, definitely. But such tenderness? No. Both Santos and Antonio were men's men, rugged, strong and definitely alpha, yet their tender, gooey centers were undeniable. A dull ache began in her chest.

Careful, girl...it's only for the weekend.

Once he'd rinsed the soap from her skin, Antonio took his turn under the spray. Taking the cloth from his hand, she returned the favor. Every limb was thoroughly washed then rinsed. She marveled over every sculpted inch of his tight body. Humming lightly under her breath, she lathered his broad chest only to be distracted by his nipples. After rinsing away the soap she licked one, the bud hardened beneath her tongue.

"You're looking for trouble, Beauty."

"And I'm pretty sure I've found it."

Smiling up at him, her tongue snaked out to lick the clean water from his chest. His face tightened and against her lower belly, his cock stirred.

Turning off the water, Antonio exited the shower. Taking a big towel he wrapped it around her. He dried her though she couldn't help but notice he wasn't as leisurely as he'd been in the shower. When he was done she wrapped a fresh towel around her body. Leaning against the vanity, she finger-combed her long hair as she enjoyed the show.

Her lover ran a towel over his body, and she enjoyed the ripple of muscle under tanned skin as he worked. His legs were long and his ass was high and tight, perfect for sinking her nails into. Where Santos was wiry, this man was muscled.

She'd found the best of both worlds.

Antonio tossed his towel on the vanity then took her hand.

"Come on."

Together they walked into the bedroom. Santos lay on the bed with a smile on his face and one hand around his semi-erect cock. Without hesitation Jane shed the towel and climbed on the bed. Crawling between his legs, she moved his hand from between his legs.

"May I?"

"As you wish." His smile was lazy.

Lowering her mouth to his cock, she ran her tongue up the

shaft. He shuddered and she repeated the motion. When her lips closed around the head, Santos bucked his hips.

Closing her eyes, Jane sank over his cock until she could take no more. Dragging her tongue along the sensitive underside, she wrapped her fingers around the base, working her fist up and down in a gentle pumping motion. His breathing took on a faint hiss.

His fingers dug into her hair as if to guide her movements, but she'd have none of it. Resisting the gentle tugs, she increased the pace. Running her tongue over the broad head, she swirled it over the narrow opening. The salty sweet taste of semen coated her tongue.

"Oh, yes."

His hips pumped in earnest now making it harder to keep the rhythm. Covering the head with her mouth, she sucked him as deeply as she could. Her hand pulsed around the shaft as she sucked him hard.

A yell was torn from him as his body arched, thrusting his cock deep in her mouth. His come struck the back of her throat, and she swallowed. Holding steady, she continued fucking him with her mouth until he went limp and his body was wracked with shivers.

Opening her eyes, she released him. Leaning forward, their lips met in a kiss so earthy that she felt the pull from deep in her pussy. Their tongues danced, and she knew he would taste his come on her tongue. Slowing the kiss, she pulled back enough to capture his lower lip between her teeth before releasing it.

"Thank you," he whispered.

"It was my pleasure."

Antonio's hands landed on her hips, and she started. She'd almost forgotten about him. Turning, she caught the need in his eyes. She moved from between Santos's legs to kneel before Antonio.

"What can I do for you?"

Between his legs, his cock was becoming stiff.

"Lie down." He patted the bed between him and Santos.

Jane acquiesced, stretching out on her back. Antonio threw his leg over her body, moving forward until his knees bracketed her shoulders. His thick cock was only a breath away from her lips, and she inhaled the scent of soap and aroused male.

"Suck me, Beauty."

The command awoke something secret within her. Something wanton and greedy. Jane faded into the shadows and Beauty, the submissive sex slave, emerged.

Opening her mouth, her tongue touched the head of his cock. He inched forward to position his cock against her lips. She opened her mouth, and his erection breached her lips. Her gaze met his, and she began sucking him. His hands fisted on the headboard and he began to thrust gently, using shallow motions as he fucked her mouth.

Santos's hand landed on her lower belly though she couldn't see him. Her tongue swirled around Antonio's cock even as Santos parted her legs. The slide of his skin against her thighs signaled his intentions. She was already wet with arousal. His breath brushed her pussy only seconds before his tongue connected with her clit. She jerked.

Her gaze was still locked with Antonio's and she tried to concentrate on sucking his cock, but it was a challenge with Santos between her thighs. His tongue was warm and wet against her sex, and she moaned deep in her throat. Two thick fingers slid deep into her pussy. Keeping up the pressure on her clit, his hand began to thrust.

Jane wasn't sure how to handle this situation. With Antonio's cock in her mouth and Santos's face in her pussy, she felt as if she were coming apart at the seams. Her hands latched onto Antonio's tight ass, her fingers dug into the muscles.

Santos's teeth slid over her clit, and she moaned around Antonio's erection. The rumble of the sound raced up her throat and straight to his cock. His eyes widened, and his hips began to thrust harder. Deep, animal-like moans sounded from his mouth and sweat broke out on his face.

Her body arched, forcing her pussy downward to put more pressure on Santos's mouth and hand. Shivers ran through her body and she felt she would fly apart at any moment. She longed for release yet she never wanted this erotic dance to end.

Under Antonio's hands, the headboard slammed into the wall. His glossy eyes slid closed, and his lips were drawn back in a grimace. He seemed to be unaware of anything other than his coming release. His groans deepened into a roar. He went rigid, his head tipped back as semen jetted into her mouth and down her throat.

Arching her back, she pressed hard on Santos. Orgasm hit her with the strength of a punch. She gave up trying to suck Antonio clean, and she let him slip from her mouth. Her screams exploded from her lungs, and her body shook.

Someone pried her hands from Antonio's ass, and the bed shifted as he moved away. Her eyes were still closed, and the remnants of her release ricocheted through her system like a pinball machine.

The torment Santos inflicted upon her was too much yet not nearly enough at the same time. His tongue swiped at her over-sensitized clit, and she tried to buck him off but he was having none of it.

A hungry mouth took possession of her nipple, and her

eyes flew open. Antonio's eyes were closed as he suckled her. Soft noises of pleasure came from him. Santos jabbed his tongue against her clit, and her body arched, wanting, needing more.

Santos rose from between her thighs. She caught a quick glimpse of his erection before he thrust it home in her cunt. His stamina was impressive. Only minutes before she'd sucked him dry, and now he was hard and ready to ride.

"Oh yes, yes!" Her fingers fisted in Antonio's hair. "Fuck me, hard. Please, please, please—"

Her sobs turned to low moans when Santos began to thrust. He moved with the enthusiasm of a teenager with quick, sharp thrusts centered on her clit.

Helpless in the face of their lust, she let go. Orgasm tore through her body stealing her breath and rocking her world. She was floating, flying in the ether with the Earth far below.

She'd been consumed.

Chapter Five

Lily was madder than hell, but she was too much of a professional to let it show. She had no idea where Jane was though she could only hope her friend was having more fun than she was.

"Did you put the champagne on ice, Richard?"

"Yes, ma'am. It is chilling and the bar has been restocked for tonight's events." He continued wiping down the bar. "The kitchen is prepping the glasses."

"Most excellent."

Lily checked several items off the list. The best part of having a well-trained staff was their ability to get set-up quickly. So far, other than running down a few items that had gone missing, this weekend was progressing well. There were only twenty more hours to go until R.S.V.P. could mark off another successful event completed.

Until then, there was work to do.

A pile of fresh table linens were stacked on a wheeled cart. Tonight's dinner was a sit down affair and the tables had to be set-up. When it was done she knew it would be exquisite with the dark burgundy tablecloths and pristine white china.

Now if the flowers would've arrived on time—

"Ms. Tyler?" Brenda, one of the waitresses, approached.

"There is a call for you on the phone across from the utility closet. It sounded quite urgent."

"Thank you, Brenda. Can you and your team get started on setting up the cocktail area on the terrace?"

"Yes, ma'am."

Lily headed into the hallway. The last time she'd been here was when she and Jean Jacques had fucked like rabbits in that closet. Her lips twisted. After their violent sex in the shower, she wasn't sure she ever wanted to see him again.

Imagine him demanding she submit to him. And then to tell her that he'd fuck anyone he saw fit until she did so, that really was the limit—

An earthy moan caught her attention, and she skidded to a halt. Standing just outside the door, the familiar sounds of sucking reached her ears.

Someone was having sex.

A trill of excitement rushed through her. As much as she loved getting laid, another favored pastime was watching others have sex. She'd barely hit puberty by the time she'd discovered this proclivity. When her parents would go out for the evening, her sister's best friend and boyfriend would come over and have sex in the den. Lily had lost count of the number of times she'd watched them screw each other's brains out.

Just the memory the boyfriend's dick pumping in and out of Leann Wilson's tight pink pussy was enough to get Lily going. It had been a long while since she'd indulged her voyeuristic side.

Holding her breath, she tiptoed closer to peer inside the closet.

A woman was on her knees before a tall man dressed in a white dress shirt. His pants were down around his ankles, and his face was hidden by an open cupboard door. His hands were fisted on the edge of the counter where Jean Jacques had fucked her not long ago. Her pussy clenched.

The woman was going down on him like he was Christmas candy. Her long black curls bounced with each forward thrust. Her scarlet lips strained around his cock, and she made greedy slurping noises.

Raising her hand, the woman wrapped it around the base of his cock. Lily caught sight of a distinctive square-cut emerald ring. A devilish thrill ran through her. It would seem that Rachel Van de Kemp used her mouth for something other than motivational speeches.

Lily had to slap a hand over her mouth to keep from laughing out loud. She could only wonder what the Denver Junior League would say about their president if they could see her on her knees with a giant cock in her mouth.

The man released his grip on the counter and reached for the woman's head. She released him, and he pulled her to her feet. Her giggle was high and girlish.

"You're such a big man," she crooned.

He didn't say anything. Taking her by the arms, they turned until she was backed against the counter. Lifting her by the waist, he deposited her on the counter then shoved up her skirt. Lily caught a flash of pale brown curls at the juncture of her thighs.

It would appear Ms. Van de Kemp wasn't a natural brunette after all.

Big Man withdrew a condom from his pocket, taking only seconds to cover his cock. Moving between her thighs, he entered her with little ceremony. Rachel didn't seem to mind as she wrapped her legs around his slim waist. His hand fisted in her shirt and with a quick tear, the front gave way as if it were tissue paper.

Memories of Jean Jacques doing the exact same thing to her in the shower sent a quiver of heat to Lily's cunt. Her thighs tightened. She would not love him. She would not—

Rachel's long moan yanked Lily's attention back to the couple. Her massive breasts were exposed—the deep brown nipples were ripe, ready to be plucked.

Fake.

"Oh my big, big man." Rachel's voice went high and shrill. "Punish me, teach me a lesson."

Lily was torn between arousal and amusement. Big Man? Teach me a lesson? It sounded like the president had watched a few too many bad porno movies.

Big Man was thrusting with slow, controlled movements. The sight of his erect cock pushing in and out of Rachel's untamed pussy was certainly arousing.

A tingle of awareness ignited in Lily's cunt. Glancing around, she darted into the phone nook directly across from the closet. Using her clipboard to shield her, she plunged her hand under her skirt and into her wet pussy.

Now Rachel leaned back, her upper body rested on her elbows. Her moans were growing in volume, and the sounds were throaty. Lily began to stroke her clit and liquid arousal gushed over her fingers. Part of her was afraid they'd all be caught while another part, her wild side, was thrilled by this unexpected development.

The slap of flesh against flesh was unmistakable. Her fingers increased their pace while her gaze remained glued on the man's ass. Tension spiraled higher and she longed for something to thrust into her pussy.

Big man's movements were less smooth and more forceful.

Thrust, flex, thrust, flex. She frowned. There was something very familiar about that butt. Thrust, flex, thrust.

He shoved his hand into his pocket and withdrew a cell phone. Laying it on the counter, it took a few seconds to realize what was going on. Her hand, still deep in her pussy, froze.

His hand came up and shoved the cupboard door closed. Lily's breath sucked in harshly when she saw his face.

Jean Jacques.

His gaze caught hers, and she felt as if all the air had been sucked out of her body. The man who'd made love to her last night was now fucking another woman.

Rachel's cries were louder and the sounds of their lovemaking were amplified by the phone in the cubby. Aghast, Lily stared at the offending instrument.

The bastard had called her to this place. He'd wanted her to see him fucking another woman.

Her gaze flew back to his face, and she ripped her hand from her panties. She recognized that look. He was going to come.

Rachel's screams peaked and the sound bounced off the walls. Jean Jacques's gaze remained locked with Lily's. Arousal, fury and naked pain warred within her heart. If she'd thought he'd hurt her before, now he'd torn her completely apart.

Picking up the phone, she slammed it down on the hook. She'd be damned before she'd watch any him come inside another woman.

Stepping out into the hallway, she tilted her chin upward. Spinning on one heel, she stalked off down the hall, rage and betrayal threatened to choke her.

That bastard! Thought he could make a fool of her did he? Well she'll just see about that.

Seconds later, Jean Jacques withdrew his cock from Rachel's hungry pussy. Even though Lily wasn't around to see him, he gave his dick a few hard jerks. With a groan, he spilled himself into the condom not wanting to share even that small part with a woman he didn't love.

Santos fed Jane a bite of sharp cheddar cheese. Her eyes closed as she savored the rich flavor that spread across her tongue. His cock stirred. Just watching her eat a simple piece of cheese made him want her all over again.

He'd lost count of how many times he and Antonio had taken her. The afternoon was a long, sensual blur of sex and release. Never had he met a woman with such a voracious appetite. He glanced over at his sleeping friend. Santos only wished he'd seen Jane first. She was the kind of woman he could almost see himself settling down with.

"Jane, tell me your fantasies." Santos stroked the curve of her jaw with one finger. "What turns you on?"

Her emerald eyes opened, and she looked toward the rumpled bed.

"I think you've already figured out that part."

"No. I want to know your deepest, darkest fantasies." He poured her a glass of champagne. "So far we've been pretty tame."

"Tame?" She laughed. "Who are you trying to kid?"

Picking up another cube of cheddar, she popped it into her mouth. Santos could barely tear his gaze from her plump lips.

"Antonio mentioned you enjoy bondage games."

"Oh, yes. I do very much."

"So, you would like us to tie you up." He ran his finger

down her throat. “And do what?”

“Well.” Her brow furrowed. A slow blush moved across her face. “You know, the usual.”

She intrigued him. Her appetites were enormous yet her sexual repertoire was somewhat limited.

“Do you want to take the submissive role?”

“Yes.”

Beneath his fingertip, her pulse increased. Her voice was slightly breathy.

“You will obey our commands?” He pulled his hand away from her.

“Yes.”

“Yes, what?”

“Yes, master.”

He liked the way she said it. Soft, needy. Even without touching her she was becoming aroused. Where had this woman been all his life?

“Do you want us to fuck you?”

“Yes.”

“Do you want us to eat your pussy?”

Her gulp was audible. Instead of speaking she nodded.

“And you will suck our cocks.”

Her tongue slipped out to dampen her lips. Heat pooled in his cock.

“When you misbehave we will spank your beautiful ass.” He leaned back, easing the pressure on his groin. “I will turn you over my knee and paddle your rear until it is bright pink.”

Her breathing hitched.

“We will enjoy paddling you.” He paused, for a moment. “I will enjoy fucking you with a dildo…or two. I believe we have some plugs around here too."

Her eyes bulged.

Santos smothered a smile. Rising, he walked to a tall secretary and opened the upper doors. A variety of sexual toys hung from hooks and were stacked on the shelves. He heard a sharp intake of breath behind him. Taking his time, he selected a pair of handcuffs and a variety of colorful scarves.

When he faced Jane, her big eyes were glued to what he held. He didn't miss the tightening of her thighs.

"Go to the bed, Beauty."

Jane scrambled out of her chair. Clutching her robe, she hustled over to stand beside the bed. As he moved closer, her knuckles turned white. Even through the thin silk her nipples created sharp little points.

This was going to be fun.

Chapter Six

Before Jane could comprehend was happening, one cuff was secured to her wrist then the other secured her hands behind her back.

"What's going on?" Antonio yawned.

"Our slave has requested we bind her and do with her what we will." Santos spoke.

"Is that so?" She heard Antonio moving in the bed. "Then I think we need to oblige."

Santos gripped the cuffs, forcing her to turn around. Antonio was still on the bed though he'd kicked off the sheets. Mischief lurked in his eyes.

"Remember," Santos's voice was deep in her ear. "If you want to stop at any time just say so. You are in charge. Do you understand?"

"Yes."

The soft whisk of metal on metal sounded near her ear before Santos's hand appeared holding a wicked looking knife. He wrapped his arms around her, the blade coming to rest against her silk covered belly.

Her knees trembled as the blade dipped behind the silk tie that held her robe closed. The blade severed the cloth with ease. Her robe opened and goose bumps broke out on her skin.

Antonio's avid gaze seared her skin and warmth blossomed between her thighs. His cock stirred.

Santos slid the blade up the sleeve, and the garment slid off one shoulder. He repeated his actions on her other arm. The cloth licked at her skin as it pooled around her ankles.

Antonio sat up. "I want you on the bed, on your knees."

With Santos's assistance, Jane climbed on the bed. It was difficult to maintain her balance with her hands behind her back, but she managed it. Once in place, she kneeled with her back to Santos. He delivered a sharp slap to her ass, and she squealed. Heat flooded her pussy.

"Keep your head down and spread your legs," Santos ordered from behind her. "I want to see your pussy."

With her feet hanging over the edge, she parted her thighs as far as she dared. Her ass stung.

"Exquisite isn't she?" Antonio spoke.

"I am without words." Santos's voice was rough. "Her skin turns pink very easily. We need to be careful not to bruise our slave."

Antonio moved across the bed until his legs bracketed hers. His engorged cock bobbed with his movements.

"You have a talented mouth, Beauty." His hand fisted around his cock and gave it a few rough jerks. Pre-come leaked from the narrow slit. "Now, suck me."

Lowering her head, she had to bend at the waist to prevent toppling over. Her mouth descended upon his cock taking him deep into her throat.

Every nerve was on high alert. Bound, she was totally at the mercy of these two men. With her hands behind her back, even if she tried to get away from them, she'd be sorely handicapped.

Antonio thrust his hips, forcing his thick cock in and out of her mouth. His hand landed on the back of her head putting him in control of her movements, her body. Her pussy clenched.

Concentrating on his cock, she sucked him for all she was worth. His taste was familiar, sexy and she wanted more of him.

More of both of them.

"I'm going to come, Beauty. And I want you to swallow every drop."

His hand fisted in her hair, and his thrusts grew more dominant. Keeping her mouth tight around his cock, her tongue swirled along the bottom of the head. He pulled her hair and it stung, still she didn't stop.

With a final jerk, a cry was torn from deep inside his throat. His come hit the back of her throat, and she swallowed. Swirling her tongue around his cock, she licked him clean before releasing him.

"She's fucking brilliant," Antonio panted.

"That she is." Santos chuckled. "And now it's my turn. Sit up, slave."

Jane straightened. He tugged on her cuffs and the right one opened. He guided her hands around to the front where he secured them again. Antonio piled pillows in front of her and when he was done, he moved back to lean against the headboard.

Keeping her gaze fixed on the duvet, Jane sank into the pillows, her cheek coming to rest on the bed. With her ass in the air and her lower abdomen braced by the pillows, she was completely exposed. Her pussy tightened.

"Now that is a sight," Antonio spoke. "Her rosy ass in the air, she looks good enough to eat, my friend."

Her pussy quivered. She was so close to the edge, it would

take little for her to come.

"It just doesn't get any better," Santos said.

She closed her eyes and buried her burning face into the duvet. Strong fingers nudged her legs further apart. His cock nudged her upper thigh as Santos spread her ass cheeks. A cool squirt of lube and he took his time smoothing the slippery gel around and inside her ass. His thick cock pressed against the tight ring, and she began to pant.

The pressure on her anus increased until her muscles gave way. The broad head slipped inside, and he paused.

"Do you want this, Beauty?" he rumbled.

She moaned into the bed.

"You need to say it, slave. Tell me you want my cock in your ass. Tell me you want me to fuck you until you come."

"Yes," her voice was muffled.

"I didn't hear you," Antonio taunted.

Santos started to pull out, and she squealed. Desperate, she thrust backward wanting to keep him inside. A sharp slap struck one cheek, and her head shot up.

"Fuck me, master. Fuck me."

Another slap landed across her ass, and she screamed. She was so painfully aroused that the sting no longer registered.

"Again," he commanded.

"Fuck me, master," she wailed.

A sharp slap struck her outer pussy lips, and she screamed. Desire tore through her flesh leaving her raw and exposed.

"Again!"

"Fuck me, master, please, I beg of you." Tears streamed down her face, and she bucked her hips toward him.

Santos thrust inside and her breath rushed from her lungs. His hand slid between her thighs and into her pussy. Slipping between the damp folds, he fingered her clit.

Every muscle in her body screamed with her need for orgasm. She shoved back, meeting him thrust for thrust. Lifting her head from the duvet, her cheeks were slick with tears. Sobs were torn from her mouth as the pressure increased.

Antonio sat against the headboard watching them. His gaze was heavy, aroused and he reached for his cock. Wrapping his hand around it, he began to stroke.

She whimpered. There was something undeniably naughty about on man fucking her in the ass while another lover watched them. She licked her lips, her body thrusting even harder against the cock in her ass and the hand in her pussy.

It was forbidden, wicked. Only in her wildest fantasies had she ever dreamed this scenario would play out, starring her.

"I'm going to come, slave," Santos rumbled. "But you may not. Not until we give you permission."

She opened her mouth to complain then Santos delivered another sharp, painful smack to her ass. Fire scorched her flesh, and she shuddered. The need for release backed off leaving her panting. She didn't know how much longer she could keep herself from coming.

Santos's hand left her pussy to latch onto her hip. His grip tightened, and his thrusts grew rough. Her pussy burned with the need to be filled. How could they torture her so?

With a final thrust, Santos buried his cock deep in her ass. He jerked, and the hot flood of his release filled her.

Antonio's cock stood at attention, his hand continuing to stroke. Her pussy ached, and she needed him to fill her. To fuck her. Her body was tense with unrealized orgasm. Behind her, Santos pulled out though she couldn't make herself move.

Gentle hands took control of her body, and she was eased onto her back. Her lashes fluttered. Santos took her cuffed hands and raised them over her head. She wrapped her fingers around the rails of the headboard.

"I'm going to eat your sweet cunt, Beauty." Antonio pushed her thighs open. "Remember, you're not to come until we tell you."

Antonio's chuckle sent shivers down her spine. Jane swallowed hard, and her pussy clenched when he bent his head. His tongue plunged into her needy flesh and she bucked, her body bowing upward. She didn't care what he did to her, just so he would allow her to come.

"How does she taste?" Santos voice sounded from somewhere to her right.

"Delicious. She's ready to come any second." Antonio pressed his finger against her clit forcing her orgasm to back down. "She can last a little while longer."

"No, I can't, please—"

"We're in charge here, slave." Santos reappeared, and he had a wicked smile on his face. "You can't come until we say you can."

"You're killing me," she hissed.

"Then you'll die of bliss."

Antonio moved from between her thighs. Reaching for her hands, he urged her to release the headboard. Santos produced the key and removed the cuffs from her wrists.

"That's better." Antonio murmured. "Now we can have some fun."

Her stomach flopped when he covered her. His big body pressed her into the bed and his thick thigh slipped between hers. She rocked her hips, desperate for anything to relieve her torment.

“She’s ready to ride,” Santos said.

“We’ll see how far this beauty can go.”

Antonio pressed his other leg between hers forcing her thighs wide. His cock rested against her hungry pussy. Desire burned deep in his eyes, and she longed to be consumed by the heat. His head dipped and his lips touched hers, once, twice.

“I want you, Beauty,” he growled against her mouth. “You make me so fucking hot I could explode just from looking at you.”

His hips rolled against hers. “Let me inside.”

Spreading her legs further, Antonio seized the moment and thrust deep. Her breath caught, and she lay there, motionless, impaled by his cock and pinned to the bed beneath him.

He withdrew only to thrust in deeper than before. The sounds that came from her mouth no longer sounded human. He continued thrusting until she writhed beneath him. With every fiber of her being she wanted an orgasm. It was so close she could almost taste it—

Without warning Antonio twisted and rolled until she was on top of him. Santos reappeared and secured her hands in the cuffs again, this time guiding her hands up and around Antonio’s neck.

Jane lay pinned to Antonio, unable to move with her arms cuffed behind his shoulders. The bed jiggled as Santos moved behind her, his big hands settling at her waist. His cock nudged at her ass, and she knew what he wanted.

Leaning into Antonio, she arched her back to give Santos better access.

Blood rushed in her ears and for a moment she felt dizzy. The insistent press of his cock against her ass brought her back to earth. Their hands seemed to be everywhere at once, and she had no choice but to give them control over her mind, body and soul.

"Easy, Beauty."

Santos pressed forward, his cock sliding into her anus. Antonio began stroking her nipples. The gentle tugs sent shivers down her back, and she relaxed into him. Santos pressed in, his cock filling her from behind. It was both pain and pleasure as he sank into her body.

Both men groaned, and Antonio's hips twitched. Her desire exploded, and she began to move. The twin cocks slid in and out of her body in mind-numbing pleasure. Antonio thrust upward, his cock hit her sweet spot dead on. Orgasm tore through her body stealing her breath and her balance. The only thing keeping her earthbound were the two men who held her captive.

Wave after wave sparked through her body and she shook. Behind her, Santos thrust and Antonio completed the movement. Inexplicably, her body responded with a gush of fluid. Exhausted, she could no more stop her hips from moving than she could prevent the sun from rising.

Her world became these two men and their magical cocks thrusting and pulling at her senses. She moaned as her body was forced up the peak again. Her arousal clawed at her flesh burning deep in her pussy.

She heard Antonio say something, but she couldn't make it out. It sounded as if he were a million miles away. A dull roar enveloped her as both men worked their cocks in and out of her voracious body.

Her heart expanded as another orgasm tore through her. She jerked helplessly in the aftermath, her body and mind no longer connected. The convulsions went on and on, each one seemed to take hours as every drop of feeling was wrenched from her body.

Antonio came seconds before Santos. Their hands burned into her flesh, and her body absorbed their liquid desire. How long she drifted on the waves of her release she didn't know.

Faintly she was aware of the men withdrawing from her. The cuffs were released and gentle hands rubbed her abraded wrists. She was eased onto the bed, and they stretched out on each side of her. There was no need for a sheet with two, healthy males in her bed.

She glanced out the French doors. The sun was creeping across the sky and the final event of the weekend was to begin at dusk. It was a lavish masquerade ball and no expense had been spared. Dozens of cases containing the finest champagne, Russian caviar, Swiss truffles, Japanese Kobe beef and fresh caught crabs and salmon from Alaska had arrived that morning.

Jane yawned. She couldn't wait to attend the ball as a very special guest would be in attendance, her ex—Peter Ellington.

Revenge would be sweet indeed.

Reinventing Jane Porter

Dedication

This one is for the readers. Thank you for your support, friendship and for encouraging me to live out my fantasy.

Chapter One

"Tell me about him."

Startled, Jane stabbed her scalp with a hairpin. Wincing, she rubbed the spot with her finger. Even without clarification she knew who Antonio was talking about. He was astute for a playboy winemaker. Then again it didn't take a Mensa candidate to know a single thirty-something-year-old woman had a skeleton in her closet.

"Who are you talking about?" Keeping her gaze fixed on the mirror, she slid the hairpin into place.

Over her shoulder, Antonio's reflection appeared in the mirror. Leaning down, he kissed her bare shoulder. The graze of his beard sent shivers across her skin. His gaze met hers in the mirror.

"You should be glad you're not an actress, Jane." His eyes twinkled. "You'd go hungry."

"Hey now, I played a tree in my third grade play." She grinned. "I was a rousing success."

"Mmm, I'll bet you were."

Spreading his legs, he straddled the end of her bench. His leather-clad legs nudged hers, and she shifted until she sat snugly between his thighs. The scent of leather and Antonio sent a lazy ribbon of warmth straight to her nipples.

Clad only in pants, he was every woman's sexual fantasy come to life. Dark hair loose about his shoulders, he was in need of a shave. Rubbing her thumb along his jaw, the abrasive hairs scraped her skin. She loved the feel of a man's stubble on her body.

"I'm asking about the man who turned you into a cynic."

"Who says I wasn't jaded before I met him?" She reached for the next pin.

"You might have been headed down that path, but I think there was one who sealed the deal."

"Talking about him is a waste of oxygen." Sliding the pin into her hair, she was pleased she'd managed to do so without drawing blood.

"That might be, but I want to know about him."

"Are you a glutton for punishment, or is this some twisted need to know who was in my bed before you?" Her gaze met his. "Trust me, my bed was cold before you came along."

"That's the least of my concerns." His eyes glinted. "You're a grown woman and of course you have a sexual past. I admit to having a healthy curiosity about the one who broke your heart."

"My heart wasn't broken."

His brow rose.

Busted.

"You're not a very good liar." The corner of his mouth hitched.

"*Pffft.*" Jane rolled her eyes. "You and Lily must've been talking behind my back."

"It didn't take more than an hour in your company to know you don't fit the profile of a woman who attends an affair such as this, *Belleza*." He shook his head. "Contrary to the signal you're putting out, you're not looking to scratch an itch."

Now it was her turn to be surprised. While she'd spent the entire day with Santos and Antonio, their conversations had been limited thanks to their sexual gymnastics.

"You're very astute, but I'm not looking for a permanent relationship." She reached for another pin.

"Maybe not right now, but that is your ultimate desire."

"Which makes me no different than most of the people here this weekend."

"Trust me," his voice dropped. "You are like none other."

"So you've been thinking about me." She began to smile. "That makes me feel all warm and fuzzy inside."

"I can't speak for Santos, but you've been the only thing on my mind since you walked into the ballroom."

"Right..."

Capturing her chin, he forced her to look at him. The look in his eye told her he was serious. Her palms began to sweat.

"I was in the gallery overlooking the ballroom when you walked in on Jean Jacques' arm. Your beautiful hair drew my attention." He twined an errant curl around one finger. "But it was your smile that held me captive."

Quivering, she held her breath as he caressed the curve of her cheek. Her nipples hardened when he stroked her lower lip with his thumb. Her breathing deepened.

"You were looking at Jean Jacques as if he'd set the sun in the sky. You were unguarded, open." His fingers traced an imaginary line along her jaw leaving only goose bumps behind.

"There was nothing false or rehearsed about you. It was a private moment between two friends, not meant to be witnessed by the man soon to become your lover."

Through her cotton chemise he touched her right nipple.

Back and forth he stroked until the tip was visible beneath the thin material.

"Seeing your body and the way you moved made me ache. Confident, sexy." His hand landed on her thigh. "You have the envious figure of a mature woman. Full breasts, hips and those long beautiful legs. All I wanted was to feel your legs locked around me." His smiled. "Or over my shoulders as I licked your sweet *coño.*"

A fine sheen of sweat dampened her skin. Listening to him left Jane's body on fire. Her pussy throbbed and against her hip his cock throbbed. Much more of this and she'd come without her *coño* even coming out to play. Gently, he began stroking her thigh with his thumb.

"But you probably knew that."

His faint smile held just a touch of shyness, leaving Jane with the urge to give him a big hug...before throwing him to the ground and fucking him into unconsciousness.

"No, I didn't."

"I've attended a few scenes—"

"Only a few?"

"—and I've learned most people are here for two reasons." His gaze moved over her face as if he was committing it to memory. "For some it's what they do. Like butterflies they move from one event to the next, and their list of lovers is extensive. Their goal is to come as much as possible and avoid emotional entanglement while doing so. Sex is their hobby, a diversion from their daily lives."

His other hand landed on her lower back. The warmth of his palm seared her skin. She felt surrounded by him, wrapped in a thick blanket of male appreciation. More than ever she felt the pull of his personality, his desire for her, and Jane wanted nothing more than to answer his call.

"On rare occasions I've met women similar to you. Beautiful, mature and confident, you know yourself and your place in the world." He shrugged. "Most women think being sexy means showing their *pechos* and the men come running..."

"Some do." Jane gestured toward her breasts. "We don't call them the orbs of power for nothing."

He shot her a quelling look.

"Even with your closest friends and family you'd lie about your sexual interests. No one in your daily life knows your darkest desires except for Lily and even she only knows what meaningless details you feed her." His hand slid up her thigh. "You enjoy the master submissive relationship, but you're not totally at ease with your desire."

Jane looked away. Their images in the mirror, so close, so intimate, sent a shudder through her body.

"You're still exploring what turns you on, and you seek to stretch your wings." The hand on her back stilled. "You prefer a monogamous relationship, one master and one submissive, but you keep your options open...for this weekend at least."

Their gazes met in the mirror, and she shivered. His desire was written on his face. She knew he was astute, but after listening to him she'd swear he was psychic. How did he come to know so much about her? Even those closest to her, people she'd known for years, didn't come close to understanding her as well.

"You're here to declare your independence. It's your time to spread your wings in the hope of regaining the confidence your former master destroyed." He gave her thigh a firm squeeze. "And when Monday morning arrives you'll return to your quiet, ordinary life and begin plotting your emergence onto the dating scene."

Lily.

Jane's heart was pounding so hard it was a wonder he couldn't feel it. The only way Antonio could know so much was if he'd talked to her friend, and she'd spilled all of Jane's business. Lily was an amazing friend, but she did have a tendency to talk too much, especially if a sexy man was the one asking the questions.

Making a mental note to strangle her business partner or worse yet, tie her up and force her to listen to country music, she smiled. That kind of torture would drive the other woman out of her mind.

"What's your point?" Looking in the mirror, she slid another hairpin into her hair.

"My point is that I pay attention, and I want to know more about you." He rose and immediately she missed the warmth of his big body. "So tell me about him."

"His name is Peter Ellington, and he's a lawyer in Denver."

"Go on."

Antonio took a seat on the foot of the bed behind her. Jane watched his reflection closely, but he gave no indication of having recognized the name. She had no doubt his brother knew Peter as he moved in the same exalted social circles as the Prentices, but Antonio was new to Denver. It was more than likely they'd yet to cross paths.

"It's really not a very exciting story." Picking up another hairpin, Jane leaned forward to examine her hair. "We met several years ago, and we dated for a while. It was no big deal."

"No big deal."

"That's what I said."

"You surprise me, Jane."

"How is that?"

Turning, it wasn't hard to see Antonio was bothered by

something. He was tense and his ready smile was gone.

"You didn't realize he was married?"

Her stomach dropped. So he did know Peter...

"Now you surprise me." She shifted her position until she was facing him. "So you've met?"

"No, but I know of him. He was recommended to me as a potential business attorney." Stretching his long legs, his bare foot nudged her ankle. The pants wore like a second skin, and she struggled to keep her attention above his waist.

"He's married with three children, all under the age of ten. Married at twenty-two, he's one of the most successful attorneys in the state. He also practices in California, and he chooses his cases based upon the possible notoriety." His smile wasn't kind. "He's a performer more than a man dedicated to his business."

"You really did your homework." She was impressed.

"You expected otherwise?"

Hot...hot...hot...

"No, I didn't."

"I don't take important decisions lightly, business or otherwise." The glint in his eye told her he wasn't talking about Peter.

"Neither do I."

Tension sizzled between them, and Jane finally looked away. He didn't have to seduce a woman when he could lure one into bed with a simple conversation. Talk about pussy-power.

She cleared her throat.

"To answer your earlier question, no, I wasn't aware he was married. It wasn't until we'd been together for almost two years that I learned the truth."

"Two years?" Disbelief colored his words.

"Being a lawyer isn't his only...talent. Mr. Ellington is also an accomplished liar, a fact I didn't learn until it was too late."

Her smile was forced. She was still mad at herself for letting Peter get past her defenses. If gold medals were awarded for kicking one's self then she'd be a champion.

"I've since learned his wife and children live a quiet life in Boulder out of the glare of the media."

"Sounds like a smart woman. Public life can be overwhelming, especially for children."

He braced his hands on the bed and the resulting ripple of his muscles caused her mind to go blank. This man should be declared illegal in at least half of the United States. Sex on two legs should not be allowed to run loose.

"How did you find out?"

She blinked. What were they talking about? Oh, yes...

"To make a long story short, on the night I'd anticipated a marriage proposal, I received an offer to become his mistress." Her smile faded. "While I didn't receive an engagement ring, he did offer me his black American Express card."

His eyes narrowed.

"I suppose the generosity of his offer was meant to be a compliment. Only I didn't quite see it that way." Looking away, she smoothed her hands along her thighs then crossed her legs. "He volunteered to pay for an apartment and all of my living expenses. Whatever my heart desired, I could just charge to his accounts. Jewelry, clothing...a new car."

Jane heard the hurt and anger in her words, but she was unable to stop the flow of anger. She began to bounce her foot.

"So while this arrangement may sound good in theory, his insistence that I make myself available to him at all hours of the day or night was the deal breaker." She waved her hand. "I mean, it would be impossible to plan meetings for the rest of my lovers when I don't know—"

Out of the corner of her eye she saw him move but before she could react, he took her chin in his hand and forced her to look at him. Their gazes clashed, and her anger was reflected in his eyes.

"He was a fool." His words were harsh. "He didn't deserve a woman such as you. He didn't know you at all did he?"

Jane was stunned by the anger resonating in his words. When he released her, she continued to gape at him.

"No, no, he didn't know me at all." Her words were little more than a whisper.

"I've only known you two days, and I understood within minutes you weren't the beck and call girl type."

He began to pace and the play of muscles beneath his bronzed skin was hypnotic. Jane forced her mind back to the conversation.

"Call girl?" She smiled.

"*Perdóname*, poor choice of words." He gave her a rueful smile. "Every now and then my English plays a trick on me."

Now that was a true gentleman. Antonio apologized for a slight slip of the tongue while Peter had insulted her to her very core and hadn't even blinked. Calling that bastard a gentleman was an insult to men of Antonio's caliber.

"No, Peter never invested the time to get to know me. To him I was a piece of ass, no more, no less." She shrugged. "He isn't terribly perceptive when it comes to women. It's a miracle he convinced someone to marry him."

Antonio chuckled.

"He's the center of his own world, the Peter-verse, and

unless a situation directly impacted him then he didn't give a damn."

"Were you in love with him?"

"I thought I was, but I realize I was fooling myself. I was more in love with the idea of him and the reality fell far short." Smiling, she shook her head. "Looking back, I know it would've been a huge mistake. Sexually I wanted to be a submissive in the bedroom, and he wanted a doormat for a companion."

"He was a stupid man who squandered the best thing to ever happen to him. I'm thankful for his *tontería*, eh, foolishness."

Antonio smiled, and Jane's cheeks heated. In the face of his compliments she was beginning to feel a little giddy. She grinned

"Fool is the least offensive term I'd use—"

"Who are you calling a fool?"

Clad only in a white bath towel, Santos exited the bathroom. His hair was damp and scattered beads of water glistened on his shoulders and chest.

Thanks to his whipcord lean physique, Jane enjoyed the play of muscles as he moved. Every movement was purposeful like a cougar readying to strike.

"We were discussing Jane's previous master." Antonio spoke.

"Anyone I know?" Santos's gaze fixed on her face.

"Peter Ellington."

A flash of recognition crossed Santos's face.

"The lawyer?" he asked.

"*Sí.*"

"So you know him too?"

Damn, is there anyone these two didn't know?

"Yes, we've met." He winked at Jane. "You didn't tell me you'd had a head injury, Jane."

Automatically her hand covered the scar on her temple. Surely Lily wouldn't have mentioned the accident to a complete stranger. Jane dropped her hand, but it was too late.

"Did he do that?" Antonio caught her wrist in a firm grip. "Did he strike you, Jane?"

Looking from one man to the other, they were staring at her so intently she felt a moment of trepidation.

"No. Well...you see...yes, I guess he did...but you have to understand...it was an accident."

"What kind of accident?" Santos edged closer.

"I was hurt and angry with him. I got a little heated. We argued, and I fell."

I sound like an idiot.

"You just fell over for no reason whatsoever?" Santos sounded skeptical.

"Yes...well...no. You see he grabbed me."

Antonio and Santos exchanged a dark look.

"I know what you're thinking." She shook her head.

Santos muttered something in Spanish, and it didn't sound like an endearment.

"You said he grabbed you?" Antonio's grip on her wrist tightened.

"You're hurting me." She winced.

"I'm sorry." He released her. "Please, go on."

"I'm not expressing myself very well." She threw up her hands. "You guys have the wrong idea."

"You said he grabbed you." Santos shot another dark look

at Antonio. "Explain this, please."

Santos practically loomed over her, and she shrank back. All vestiges of the urban gentleman were gone, leaving an angry man who looked ready to throw down. It was funny how intimidating he could look dressed only in a towel.

"Yes, he did grab me but you have to understand it was an accident." Jane's heart was beating so rapidly her head was starting to feel swimmy. "When he asked me to be his mistress—"

"Mistress?" Santos's nostrils flared and his eyes held a dangerous glint. "He wanted you as his *puta*?"

"He didn't tell her he was married." Antonio leaned toward Santos and spat something in guttural Spanish. Lily didn't know what he said, but it didn't sound complimentary.

"*Bastardo*," Santos hissed.

That word she knew.

"Listen, both of you." She rose and held up her hands. "When he propositioned me I was upset. We argued and when he tried to stop me from leaving—"

"It doesn't matter what you did, Jane. Even if you gave him a black eye, no man should raise a hand toward a woman." Antonio captured her hands. "Any man who does so deserves an old fashioned ass-kicking."

"Name the time and place and I'll be there." Santos's hands fisted.

"Neither of you will do any such thing." Jane pulled away from Antonio. "Whatever happened between Peter and me is over, finished. There is no need for retribution. I've moved on."

"*Belleza*." Santos took her in his arms. "When our woman is disrespected, you must allow us to be angry for your sake. We're men, it's what we do."

"I don't approve of violence." Stiff in his embrace, she looked from Santos to Antonio then back again. "Do you understand?"

"My English...not so good," Santos teased.

She slapped him on the chest, and he laughed.

"*Amigo*, our Jane has claws. I think we need to keep her."

Keep me?

Santos pulled her closer, and she melted into his arms. His scent was a pleasing combination of soap and male skin. Inhaling deeply, she laid her head against his chest. Antonio stepped behind her, his hands landing on her shoulders. Surrounded by both men she realized she'd never felt as treasured as she did in that moment.

"Every now and then we men like to drag our knuckles on the ground," Antonio whispered in her ear. "It's good to bring out the caveman."

She began to laugh. Turning, she slid an arm around each of their waists until she was cuddled between two rock hard chests. She was the luckiest woman in the entire house.

Chapter Two

If that bitch doesn't keep her hands off his ass, I will tear out her dollar ninety-nine weave.

Slamming steak knives into a divided tray, Lily glared at her erstwhile lover. Standing in the center of the ballroom, Jean Jacques was surrounded by three fawning blonde women. All of them possessed the same simpering, star-struck look as if he'd created chocolate for them alone.

With their fake nails and nerve-shredding giggles, it was all Lily could do to refrain from walking over to them and beating them to a pulp. Of course doing so would make her look like a jealous hag and that she couldn't have.

Combat rule number one, never let the enemy know what you're feeling.

What she really wanted to do was smack them over their collective blonde heads with an oversized baseball bat emblazoned with "Get a CLUE". No woman should make over a man like they were. Her lips twisted. She'd die before she'd ever do it.

Jean Jacques smiled, and the ladies burst into a chorus of high-pitched giggles. They were petting him like he was a dog.

Her gaze narrowed. She'd bet her best pair of Jimmy Choo's there wasn't a dry panty among them. The shortest woman turned and thanks to her sheer white pants, it was obvious the only thing she wore was lotion and a smile.

Snatching up another handful of knives, she dropped them into the tray with a clatter. Watching the Barbie trio simpering up at Jean Jacques was making her nauseous—

You'd be doing the same thing if you were standing with him.

"Fat chance," she muttered.

Sucking in a noisy breath, Lily was struck with a horrifying thought. Had she ever watched him with such complete adoration? Even worse, were there witnesses?

Eww.

Her scowl deepened. She certainly hoped not as her reputation would be in shreds. Lily wasn't the kind of woman who drooled over any man no matter how handsome he was. She'd learned early on everyone had clay feet, and she would live a lifetime of bad footwear before she would grovel at any man's feet.

No man, no matter how well hung, was worth public humiliation.

Besides, one of her favorite hobbies was making fun of women who acted like the Barbie triplets. She was far too old to change her ways.

No, the men came to her, they always had. From the moment her breasts exploded through her one and only training bra, the boys weren't far behind. Of course, having an older sister built like a stripper had helped. Anna's escapades taught Lily that sex, used correctly, made an excellent leash for any man she chose.

For Lily, sex was about the chase rather than the in-out-in-out. Men loved nothing more then getting a woman naked and, if said woman knew how to prolong the game, it was almost as exciting as the physical act. Anticipation was the ultimate foreplay.

A shriek of laughter caught her attention. The tallest Barbie with the bad weave and ginormous breasts laid her hand on his arm. She was wiggling like a happy puppy, and her rock hard boob kept hitting him in the side.

Damn, she'd better not break one. They'd all drown.

Jean Jacques didn't seem to be bothered by the surplus of female attention directed his way. Hell, he was eating it up. Even from twenty feet away she heard the familiar cadence of his voice. Though she couldn't hear what he was saying, the bimbettes hung on every syllable.

And you think you wouldn't be staring up at him like that?

Like hell.

Lily gripped the tray until her knuckles turned white. The bastard should come with a warning label: When with this man, consider your panties and peace of mind to be at risk.

The shortest sycophant put her hand on his other arm. Her breasts were in danger of spilling out of her too-small corset, but at least they looked real. She rubbed against him as if he was catnip, and she was a pussy looking for a buzz.

"Tramp." She forced herself to release her grip in the tray for fear she'd throw it at their heads. "Why don't you just strap a mattress to your back and advertise your intentions?"

"Ah, Lily, how I have missed your sweet disposition."

She knew that voice. Robert Armand, one of Dirk's senior managers stood behind her. Dressed in his usual black from head to toe, his smile was wide. No doubt her former lover was amused at catching her unawares.

"Hmm, I don't remember you on the guest list." She picked up her clipboard and feigned checking the guest list. "I thought you were in Europe slumming with the French."

"I would hardly call it slumming especially after living in one of the best Parisian hotels for more than six months." His eyes twinkled. "I'm not sure I remember how to make my own coffee.

"I'm sure you'll manage." Lily threw her arms around him and gave him a big hug. "You're a far better cook than I."

"That is hardly a compliment from a woman who believes tinned beans with hot dogs is a delicacy."

"Hey, I learned how to work a microwave while you were gone."

"Mmm, now you can warm the beans first." He nodded toward Jean Jacques. "I don't think I've ever seen you jealous over another woman."

"Me? Jealous of what?" Ignoring her burning cheeks, she waved her hand in the direction of the Barbies. "Too much Lycra and peroxide poisoning? No thanks."

"You're out of practice, Lily. You were a much better liar six months ago." Robert chuckled. "Admit it. Your panties are in a twist because our friend over there has always had a hard-on for you and right now, you don't even exist. You can lie to yourself all you want but deep down, you and I both know I'm right."

Smug bastard.

She'd always hated that she'd allowed Robert to get to know her so well. They'd dated for three months before realizing they made better fuck-buddies than boyfriend and girlfriend. Ever since then they'd hooked up when he was in town and spent a few nights of rough and tumble, get your skirt dirty...sex. The pillow talk afterward gave him an insight into her personality that few others had.

His ability to assess a situation and call it like it was, was one of many reasons why Dirk valued him so much. Personally, she liked him better when his mouth was otherwise occupied...

"Sometimes I think I hate you." She spoke without heat.

"I don't believe it. From time to time you would like to think you do, but I know better. We're too much alike, so if you hate me, you're really hating yourself." He smiled. "Besides, who else could keep you on the straight and narrow?"

"Woo-hoo, how did I ever survive without you?" She rolled her eyes.

"Cheer up, Lily." Robert dropped his arm around her shoulders. "It could've been worse if I'd had a twin."

"I'm thankful for small mercies." She groaned.

"That's my girl."

Her gaze drifted to Jean Jacques. He was so damned handsome with his chiseled features and rock hard body. For two years they'd resisted their mutual attraction. They'd fought, teased, tormented and laughed together, and she knew they couldn't ever go back to what they were less than twenty-four hours ago.

Jean Jacques put his arm around one of the women, and Lily felt as if her chest went hollow. She felt his loss more keenly than she'd ever dreamed she could. She'd gotten used to his gaze following her when he thought she wasn't paying attention. Secretly she enjoyed how he would compliment her on what she wore.

The best part was he would open doors for her and as she walked through, he would place his hand on her lower back. Each and every time she thought her knees would buckle when he touched her there.

When Jean Jacques was near, her reaction was strong and

immediate. Just hearing his voice caused every hair to stand on end and if they were face to face, her nipples hardened every time. She'd come to realize that on some level she'd already claimed Jean Jacques as her own.

Her shoulders sagged.

Right now the emotional chasm between them was wider than mere distance could ever be.

The tall Barbie's hand landed on his abdomen as she spoke. The flash of her red nails against his white shirt was like waving a red cape in front of a bull.

"I'm going to snatch that bitch bald, Robert." Her fists clenched.

"Lily, you've nothing to be jealous of." Robert's lips touched her ear. "Those women don't possess any of your enviable talents. The woman whose hair you're threatening—she's the governor's daughter. She graduated last year and announced that her greatest desire in life is to be a trophy wife."

"Somehow that doesn't surprise me. I never suspected she'd set her sights so...high." Sarcasm dripped from every syllable.

Robert laughed, and she ignored him. Lily was pissed and not in the mood to be teased into a smile. Not only had she let a man get under her skin, but it was Jean Jacques, the one she'd promised herself she couldn't have. Years of self-restraint thrown out the window for sex.

Well, really, really great sex...the best sex she'd ever experienced.

"Feeling insecure?" Robert gave her a one-armed hug. "You're ten times more woman than those girls could ever hope to be." His voice dropped, and his breath caressed her ear. "And far more desirable."

A slow tingle ignited in her lower belly. Robert, like Jean Jacques, had some serious charisma. Both men had an indefinable aura that never failed to flip any woman's switch. It was one of several reasons why her relationship with Robert was so enjoyable. They both appreciated good wine, classical music and hot sex, the raunchier the better.

She shot a dark look at Jean Jacques. So unlike a certain Frenchman, being with Robert was easy, comfortable. She looked up at him.

"I'm not in love with him."

His brow rose. "I never said you were."

"And if he prefers a Ford to a Jaguar—" she jerked her head toward Jean Jacques and the Barbies, "—that's his loss."

"That's my girl." His smile was encouraging. "Sometimes you need to be reminded that you're in charge. If you want him, take him. While Jean Jacques may be flirting with other women..."

"He fucked another woman in front of me." The moment the words were out, her eyes began to sting.

"Wow." His gaze roamed her face. "That's a twist. What the hell did you do to him?"

"Me?" She pushed him away. "I didn't do anything."

"Lily, stop." His voice was gentle. "Here's how I see it."

Gripping her shoulders, he forced her to turn toward Jean Jacques and the Barbies.

"You love him—"

She snorted.

"—and I'm pretty sure he loves you. You've allowed you pride to dictate what you say, but it's not how you feel on the inside." His hands landed on her hips. "Not every male in the universe is a complete dick, and Jean Jacques, he's one of the good ones."

"Yeah, right—"

Lily started to turn away, but Robert's grip tightened.

"I don't know why he had sex with another woman, but if you don't wake up and swallow some of that damnable pride then you're going to destroy the best thing to ever happen to you." His voice dropped to a whisper. "You've outgrown your capricious life, Lily. Even Holly Golightly had to grow up sometime."

Her heart ached and now her eyes burned. She knew Robert was right but her pride, her damned wonderful, hateful pride wouldn't allow her to admit it.

"It's always been Jean Jacques for you." His voice grew husky. "I introduced the two of you, remember? Both of you looked as if you'd been struck by lightning. Even if I'd been in love with you it would've been over right then. Not once did you look at me as you did him."

Damn, there had been a witness!

"Have you been reading romance novels again?" Her nails dug into her palms, but the pain was nowhere near the growing ache in her chest. "You always get sappy when you do."

"Only the sexy bits." He chuckled. "I need to keep myself occupied in the darkest hours of the night or else I will go out and have sex with inappropriate women."

"I'm not falling for it. Every eligible woman in your Paris hotel probably ended up in your bed."

"Not quite." His lips touched her neck. "There was a transgender female who worked in the laundry, and she was the only one to avoid my bed."

"You probably nailed her on a washing machine."

His hand skimmed over her hip to the top of her thigh. Her

pulse leapt. Even though she was in love with Jean Jacques, Robert still had the ability to jump-start her libido. Old habits died hard.

"Sorry to disappoint you, but she turned me down." His teeth grazed her earlobe. "It would seem she'd become a woman only to turn lesbian."

She began to laugh.

"Keep it up, Lily. Your lover is getting restless now that my hands are all over you." His tongue tickled the indentation behind her ear. "Do you think making him jealous would help to appease your hurt feelings?"

"You're getting warm." She tilted her head to the side.

"Being a man gives me some insight into how the male mind works." He tugged her earlobe with his teeth. Her nipples hardened. "If I were to guess, I'd say our friend fucked another woman to deliberately hurt you."

Lily thought about how she'd accused him of screwing another woman before he'd carried her out of the ballroom and into the utility closet. If he was innocent, her accusation would've taken a chunk out of his hide.

"You could be right."

"Our boy is possessive, very possessive. Seeing you with another man will drive him insane." His breath was hot on her shoulder. "Your man has definite ideas when it comes to his women and another man invading his territory is an insult he cannot ignore."

"What do you get out of this?" Lily hissed. "You work with him, won't this interfere with business."

"Hell, no." His chest shook against her back. "I owe the bastard for fucking my assistant last summer. I'd asked her to dinner at least a dozen times, and she turned me down. That bastard waltzed in and had her naked on my desk within an hour. Making him watch me fuck you will be the highpoint of my year."

Don't do it...

"Why Robert, I like how you think."

Tilting her head, she watched Jean Jacques through her lowered lashes. He wasn't looking in their direction, but his demeanor had certainly changed. The smile was gone and judging from the tightness of his jaw he could very well be grinding his teeth.

Poor boy, you are so screwed.

"Besides, who knows when we'll have this chance again?" Robert said. "Once both of you get over your stubborn pride, our relationship will be over."

"I am a one-man kind of woman."

His hand dipped beneath her waistband and made a beeline south. Widening her stance, Robert didn't hesitate to accept her invitation. Slipping into her panties, he cupped her pussy.

"Fuck, Lily, I want to strip you bare and take you on the bar."

She moaned when his fingers delved into her cunt. Clutching his arm, she rose onto her tiptoes to give him better access.

"Only feet away your lover is flirting with nameless, faceless women." Two fingers invaded her pussy, and she quivered. "I'm inside you, but it's his fingers your body remembers."

He began to thrust. Arousal washed over her and when his thumb stroked her clit, her legs began shaking. She was grateful for his arm or she would melt to the floor.

"Your pussy is so hot I could fuck you all day, Lily."

"You've already done that." She laughed.

"Indeed I have."

Jean Jacques was staring at them, and he did not look happy. Good. Reaching back, her fingertips stroked Robert's firm jaw. Her hips began to move, leaving Jean Jacques in no doubt as to what was happening behind the bar.

Still surrounded by the Barbies, he'd given up any pretense of paying attention to the women. Her gaze met his and her chin came up, silently daring him to say or do anything to stop her.

A muscle began to tick in his jaw when Robert's free hand covered her breast. He stroked her nipple and she covered her hand with his. Soft whimpers tumbled from her lips as liquid heat washed through her pussy. Jean Jacques' darkening expression only added to her arousal.

"You're so tight, hot." The pace of Robert's hand increased. "Let him see your passion, your fire."

Driven by the twin devils of Robert's hand and Jean Jacques' anger, she arched, pressing her rear into Robert's pulsing crotch. Tossing back her head, she no longer cared who was watching. Her need for release overrode everything else, even revenge.

But it wasn't to be.

Robert released her, and she stumbled. She turned and he took her by the shoulders, forcing her backward until she was half-sitting on the edge of the beer cooler. His massive erection prodded her belly.

"You should get dressed for tonight." Slowly, deliberately, he skimmed his hands down her body. "You're officially off duty, Ms. Tyler."

"But, I still have—"

"No, you don't."

Catching the hem of her skirt, he pulled it up to her hips. His blue eyes gleamed, and he lowered himself to his knees. Gaping at him, she began to shake when she realized what he was about to do.

Spreading her legs, Robert lifted each one over his shoulders. Her hands slammed down on the cooler when he balanced her weight on his shoulders. Spreading her pussy lips, his tongue touched her clit and her body jerked.

Lily was both thrilled and appalled when he set to work. Robert was a pussy-eating fool. Many times he'd joked about packing a lunch and spending the day between her thighs. And on more than one occasion he'd done just that.

"Oh, yes, yes!" Her head tipped back.

His tongue was warm, firm as his fingers slid deep into her cunt to focus on her G-spot. Her eyes rolled back into her head as wave after wave of need burned through her system. Her soft moans grew to howls of need and her hips rocked on the edge the cooler.

"Harder...yes, just like that. Yes, yes, yes!"

Leaning her back against the bar, her body arched upward when her release struck. Wave after wave of pulsing release tore through her body leaving her breathless and shaking. Robert withdrew his hand and every nerve screamed in protest. Her mind whirled and her greedy cunt cried for more even as he slid her thighs from his shoulders.

With his damp fingers, he outlined her lips with the juice from her pussy. Unable to resist, her tongue slipped out to taste her arousal. The salty flavor made her toes curl.

"Now, go upstairs." Robert's smile was enigmatic. "Your task, should you choose to accept, is to teach Jean Jacques how to treat a lady."

"Mmm."

"And when you walk out of this room, don't you dare look back." His lips touched hers. "Your lover has reverted to Cro-Magnon form and his brow ridge is growing heavier with each passing minute."

Sliding an arm around her waist, Lily felt boneless when he helped her to her feet. His hands skimmed her thighs moving her skirt back into place. Keeping her gaze down, she turned to retrieve the silverware tray she'd filled.

A wash of cool air caressed her ass and she realized it had been a mistake to turn her back. His hand struck one cheek and the sharp sound of flesh on flesh echoed through the ballroom. A flood of need washed through her pussy, and she moaned. Her knees wobbled and it was the sound of a female voice that prevented her from sliding to the floor.

"Wow. Do you think I can be next?"

Lily's cheeks burned and for the first time in her life she wanted to run away. If she'd been anyone else she might've done it. But Lily Tyler never ran no matter the situation and now was not the time to start.

Picking up the tray, she threw Robert a heated look. The marble expanse of the ballroom never looked wider than it did in that moment. Tray in hand, she crossed the ballroom and deposited it where the setup crew would find it.

When she slipped through the swinging doors, Lily breathed a sigh of relief. Alone, she broke into a run toward the stairwell.

Not only had Robert called her jealous, he'd then given her a screaming orgasm before an audience including the man she was in love with. And if that wasn't bad enough, he'd spanked her on the ass.

Her heels clattered on the steps, and she was out of breath

when she reached the top. Opening the door, she peered into the second floor corridor. It was empty.

She bolted down the hall then dove for the door to her suite. Her fingers felt thick as she fumbled with the lock. When she finally managed to get it open, she threw herself inside and slammed the door taking a few seconds to secure the lock again. Leaning her forehead against the solid oak, she struggled to catch her breath.

Torn between the desire to laugh or weep, she began to shake. Not only had she caught her lover with another woman, he'd then been a witness to her public debauchery. She groaned. What as she thinking?

Her legs were shaking so hard she allowed herself to crumple to the floor. Wrapping her arms around her knees, she bowed her head, allowing her tears to run free.

Lily wasn't sure what was more shocking, a public orgasm or being spanked on the ass and liking it.

Chapter Three

"*Copia.*" Santos was looking out the window, one finger on the tiny headset in his ear. "Ellington has arrived."

"*Pobre bastardo.*"

Antonio secured a red silk sash around his waist with a jerk. Since hearing Jane's story, the anger he felt was like a sleeping beast in his gut. Upon scenting his prey, the creature was coming back to life and the need to feed the anger was growing. Their woman, for all of her protests, had been hurt by this lawyer and a price needed to be paid...in blood.

"...eye on both of them and if you see anything suspicious, notify me immediately."

Momentarily diverted, Antonio frowned at Santos. What was going on?

"*Gracias.*" The other man turned away from the window. "Ellington's escort is none other than the beautiful Giselle." Santos's mouth firmed. "That's how she got past security last night. Even though he was out of town, she used his invitation and attended as his guest."

"She's nothing if not predictable." Antonio shook his head. "She's returned to her own kind, the bottom feeders."

"And in doing so, she's saved an untold number of unsuspecting men from a woman with only one thing on her mind."

"Money." They spoke in unison.

"So what's the plan, *amigo*?" Santos slapped him on the shoulder. "A healthy dose of public humiliation? We could go old school and deal with him man to man." He cracked his knuckles, a feral smile formed. "Maybe an old-fashioned fist fight? I would enjoy some blood-sport this evening."

His friend might appear to be an urbane, sophisticated man of the world but Antonio knew the truth. At a tender age, Santos had been left to fend for himself in the crowded backstreets of Barcelona, fighting for every scrap of food he put in his mouth. His days of using his body as a means to survival came to an abrupt end when he had attempted to pick the pocket of Antonio's grandfather. Street-wise and compassionate, Enrique Villareal snatched the boy from the streets and had brought him to the vineyard to live.

He'd been a half-wild child with no understanding of how polite society operated. It took many long months of patience and unwavering love before Santos had come to understand he no longer needed to steal or sell his body to survive.

Slowly the rage of a child abandoned, abused, had been eroded with generous meals, a room to call his own and a family who adored him. He had worked hard at the vineyard and took to his school lessons with a passion. At thirty-one he held a master's degree in business, and he was Antonio's right hand in the business.

Despite everything Santos had accomplished, the street urchin from Barcelona still lurked beneath the Italian suits and flawless grammar. On many occasions Antonio witnessed the veneer dissolve and the fighter emerge and it was a fearsome sight.

Antonio hoped for Ellington's sake that Santos kept his

wits about him long enough to avoid breaking him in half.

"Both of us would enjoy beating that bastard into the ground, but we need to approach this carefully. We don't want to upset Jane. We'll let Ellington make the first move."

"And Giselle?"

"Leave her to me. She and I have unfinished business." Antonio held up his fist. "Agreed?"

"*Sí.*" Santos knocked his knuckles against Antonio's. "I only hope the lawyer has his health insurance paid up."

They began to laugh, the tension eased. But their merriment died when the bathroom door opened and Jane exited. Antonio's breath caught.

Her golden hair was arranged in a complicated series of waves and curls studded with blue and white crystals. A pale blue velvet collar studded with more crystals encircled her slim throat. Her sky blue silk corset created a bounty of cleavage and her nipples were saved from overexposure by a thick ruffle of white lace.

The matching skirt was miniscule in the front, barely covering the apex of her thighs. They'd forbidden her to wear panties and it would only take a slight breeze or the touch of a curious finger to expose her pussy.

With a tapered hem, the back of the skirt came down to create a short train. Six-inch platform stilettos made her already long legs seem even longer and more graceful. Every inch of her body had been pampered and groomed for this evening. From the top of her head to her pale blue toenails, Jane Porter was every man's hottest fantasy come to life.

And she was theirs.

Antonio's cock hardened. The desire to take her beneath him rose hot and heavy. He glanced at Santos. His friend looked as stunned as he felt.

"Well? How do I look?" She sounded breathless. "Okay?"

"Stunning." Antonio approached and took her hand. "Every man will fight for the pleasure of looking upon you."

"Thank you, kind sir." Her curtsey was quick and her cheeks were flushed with pleasure. "You're looking mighty handsome yourself."

"Standing next to you no one will even notice me." Raising her hand to his mouth, he kissed her knuckles.

"I doubt that." Her gaze met Santos's.

"Santos?"

"*Belleza*, I am beyond words."

He joined them and with one finger he brushed a stray hair from her shoulder. When his skin touched hers, Antonio felt the quiver that ran through her. Her breathing hitched and her pink tongue darted out to dampen her lips. A searing shaft of arousal tore through his lower belly. He released her hand.

"I have a feeling we'll spend most of our evening fighting off her admirers." Antonio laid a hand on Santos's shoulder.

"You could be right." Santos shot him a faux-serious look. "Do you think we should mark her? No man will be left in doubt as to who her masters are."

Antonio pretended to consider the idea. Jane's eyes were wide and her breathing fast. Her hands smoothed the front of the corset coming to rest on her lower belly. White teeth worried the tender flesh of her lower lip.

"I think we should. It will save us wear and tear on our knuckles." Antonio shot Santos an amused glance.

"Excellent point. What shall we use? A paddle?" Santos moved around Jane, not touching her but leaving no doubt of his intentions. After circling her twice, he gestured toward the bed. "A shiny pink bottom will serve as a warning to any man who covets our woman. Go, Beauty, take your place."

Turning, Antonio opened the doors to the toy armoire. The array of sex-oriented toys was modest—paddles, crops, handcuffs crafted from a variety of materials, ropes and other essentials were neatly lined up in hooks or on the shelves. He'd always considered himself a purist when it came to sex, and battery operated gadgets need not apply. He preferred his partners to achieve orgasm through their play, not technology.

Removing a medium-sized leather paddle from the armoire, he admired the workmanship. He'd picked up this little toy in Brussels weeks before coming to America. One side was leather and the other was covered in thick, soft felt. Rubbing the padded side against his palm, he was sure Jane would enjoy his latest purchase. He closed the doors.

Their slave was on her knees on the bench at the foot of the bed. Her torso was resting on the bed leaving her bare ass at the perfect angle for a proper spanking. Her figure was ideal for bondage. With her generous breasts and slim waist, she was born to wear corsets. Add in her rounded hips and generous ass, and Jane could be the poster girl for submission.

"I want to see your pussy." Santos stood behind her. "Spread those legs."

Without hesitation Jane did as he'd instructed. Her back arched just enough to expose her glistening labia. She was primed and ready to play.

"Tonight is a milestone for you, Jane." Antonio fingered the paddle. "You'll make your debut as our slave, and you'll be known only as Beauty. When you leave this room, Jane Porter will cease to exist."

"Yes, master," she whispered.

Laying his hand at the base of her spine, he realized she

was trembling. Trepidation only added to her arousal, it was good that she was afraid.

"I'd like you to meet my new friend." He ran the soft side of the paddle over her rear. "A little toy I picked up a few weeks ago, and I haven't had the opportunity to break it in yet. I hope you'll enjoy it."

Flipping it over, he spanked her with the leather side. Startled, she jerked.

"We did not give you permission to move, *Belleza*." Santos cupped his hand and gave her a firm swat on her rear. "We are your masters, and we'll tell you what to do and when to do it. Your thoughts are no longer your own as our pleasure is now yours."

"Yes, master."

"This evening you will see to our pleasure." Antonio rubbed the soft side of the paddle down her thigh then up again. "We will never ask you to do anything that will humiliate or harm you. Do you understand?"

"Yes, master."

"Everything we do is for you, Beauty." He drew the paddle over the curve of her ass. "If you please us then you will be greatly rewarded."

"And if you fail, the punishment will be swift and harsh." Santos spanked her again, this time with the flat of his hand.

"Yes, master."

Antonio flipped the paddle around and brought it down. The smack on flesh was satisfyingly loud. As he guided the paddle to strike her buttocks and thighs, her skin grew warm and rosy. With each spank her cries escalated and her hips thrust so far back her wet pussy was fully exposed.

"That is a sweet cunt, my friend. Half of the men

downstairs would give their right arm for a taste of her." Santos's tone held no more interest than if he were talking about the weather. "We are but two men. Would it be bad form to keep her all to ourselves?"

"Do you think we should share her?"

"Mmm, the idea is tempting." Santos was grinning. "Watching our slave pleasure another man could be quite arousing."

Antonio brought the paddle down across her pussy. Her response was sharp and immediate. A woman who didn't hesitate to express herself in bed was a definite turn on.

"We don't normally share our slaves but I'll admit, the idea of watching *Belleza* suck a strange man's cock is making my dick hard." Grabbing the front of his pants, Antonio sought to alleviate the pressure on his engorged cock. He'd be lucky if the buttons of his fly weren't imprinted along one side.

"*Belleza*, we would like to display you this evening." Santos touched her ankle. "Have you done this before?"

"No, master."

Heat surged through his body, and Antonio brought the paddle down again. Her cream trickled down her thigh and her ass was bright pink. Her hips rocked as if she were fucked by an invisible man. The sensual stretch and arch of her back was mesmerizing and it was all he could do not to tear open his pants and thrust inside her.

Turning the paddle, he ran it over her blushing flesh. Tonight was important, though not for the reasons Jane believed. They would put her on display in the ballroom and allow strangers to touch and fondle their submissive. Her unveiling would bring down the house and, most importantly, force Peter Ellington to show himself.

Chapter Four

Jane wasn't sure she would be capable of walking if it wasn't for Santos and Antonio on either side. Their linked arms served to keep her upright and moving forward. Her legs were still wobbly, and her ass stung from the paddling she'd received. Her thighs were still sticky with her cream, and they'd refused her request to wash up.

The toe of her shoe caught on the carpet. Both men looked down at her, and she smiled. Normally she didn't wear heels but Lily had talked her into buying the ridiculously high shoes. She'd protested but the other woman had been adamant.

She was getting used to them and she had to admit, they did make her feel sexy. Her walk had a little extra shimmy, drawing attention to her breasts and ass. With each step cool air licked at her damp cunt. Anticipation vibrated along her skin standing every hair on end.

The thought of being displayed was exhilarating and scary. She'd witnessed the spectacle of submissives arranged like statues while others stopped to admire them. Her pussy pulsed. It wasn't unusual for someone to touch the displays though etiquette required they ask permission from the slave's master first.

It was funny, but she trusted the two men who walked beside her though they were little more than strangers.

Intimate strangers.

She had no doubt they would keep their word and watch out for her. They would allow nothing to go awry while they were on watch.

“Here we go,” Santos murmured. His hand covered hers.

The hallway outside the ballroom was crowded with waitstaff and guests. Even though her costume was the most scandalous she'd ever worn, once again she was demure in comparison to the other ladies.

Many of the women were topless, and she'd never seen such an array of body piercings. Nipples adorned with metal bits, all shapes and sizes imaginable. A redhead with a cat headband and very little else was showing off her pussy piercings. Jane's eyes widened when she spied multiple pieces of metal jutting from her flesh.

One word, OUCH.

Many of these people were current or future clients, which made her doubly grateful for the masks. Jane wasn't sure she could discuss the merits of a sit down dinner over a buffet knowing her client had a devil charm hanging from her labia.

The ballroom was dark and as crowded as the hall. Some sort of European techno music thundered from a sound system on the stage. A small dance floor was crowded to overflowing with gyrating bodies in all shapes and colors imaginable. The overhead lights had been changed to strobes of blue, pink and red giving it a club atmosphere.

To the left was an informal arrangement of couches and chairs. Piles of big pillows and oriental carpets invited people to sit on the floor if they chose. Behind one of the couches stood three slaves, one male and two females with their hands braced on the back and their asses thrust out.

The blonde female was being spanked by a tall man

dressed in a leather jock strap. Despite the roar of the music, Jane could hear the other woman's moans.

The male slave had his legs spread and his head down. His mistress, a woman in a dark red dress and feathered mask, held a fat anal plug in one hand and a tube of lube in the other. After greasing the plug, she handed it to the third slave.

The young woman spread the man's ass cheeks to expose his rosy hole. Pressing the thick plug against the tight ring of muscle, she didn't let up until his anus opened under the force. Sweat gleamed on his skin. Inch by delicious inch his greedy hole devoured the plug until only the thick base was visible.

His mistress reached for the exposed base and gave it an experimental twist. The man swore even as his hips thrust forward. She scolded him then gave him a quick crack across the ass with her hand. His head came up and the flash of pleasure pain on his face was enough to elicit a rush of cream to Jane's pussy.

I don't think I'm in Kansas anymore.

She allowed her men to lead her away. The submissives were easy to spot as they wore the least amount of clothing. Almost all of them sported some sort of collar with leashes attached. Their masters carried the leashes firmly, tethering their slaves to their sides.

Many of the males sported costumes of Roman noblemen, cowboys, police officers and more than a few cavemen. While some of them were pretty hot, none of them could compare to her escorts. Both were dressed as pirates complete with flowing shirts and swords. Antonio looked as if he'd stepped off the cover of a romance novel while Santos was clad all in black. The only spots of color were the gold hoops on each ear.

As they wove their way through the crowd, her eyes widened when she saw their destination. Near the dance floor, an elaborate structure resembling a cage had been constructed. Pedestals of varying heights were arranged under the canopy and submissives, mostly women, stood on them posed like statues. A variety of restraints dangled from the overhead canopy though not all of the slaves used them. Some stood as if they were modeling for a catalog while others were contorted into positions Jane had thought impossible to accomplish without serious spinal damage.

Armed with glasses of champagne, spectators walked among the living statues admiring them under the watchful eyes of their masters. Several people were touching the women, a nipple tweak here, a pussy stroke there.

She quivered.

"Does this arouse you, *Belleza*?" Santos whispered in her ear.

Unable to speak, she simply nodded. Her throat was tight and her skin felt as if it had shrunk two sizes. Her sex pulsed with the beat of the music, and her need for release increased.

Antonio led them to an unoccupied pedestal closest to the wall. Her heart was pounding when he released her arm. Turning, his face was mostly covered by his mask and the only sign of life was the gleam of his eyes.

"Please remove your skirt, *Belleza*. You will pose for our friends."

For a moment she was frozen, unable to move or breathe. Her lungs ached and spots wavered in her vision. When Santos released her arm, she sucked in a noisy breath.

I'll be okay…

Her hands shook when she released the clasp on her skirt. She would bet her ass cheeks were as pink as the woman's she'd seen being spanked. The velvet licked at her skin when the clasp gave way. Handing the garment to Santos, she took

Antonio's hand. Using him for balance, she stepped up onto the pedestal.

"Put your hands behind your back."

Her knees began to shake when she felt the kiss of silk at her wrists. He bound her hands behind her back taking care to ensure her restraints weren't too tight.

"*Belleza*, we'll be less than two feet away." Santos's voice was meant for her alone. "No one will overstep their bounds."

"Thank you," she whispered.

"You're welcome." She caught the flash of his teeth when he smiled.

"Bend down a bit, Beauty. With nipples as beautiful as these, everyone should be allowed to admire them."

Antonio teased her breasts from the confines of the corset. The stiff lace scraped the tender buds, and her breath caught when the friction sent a jolt of heat to her core. She gasped when he shot her a heated look before taking possession of a nipple. Santos took the other and together the forceful sucking tore a strangled moan from her mouth. She swayed and strong hands held her in place until the moment passed.

"Let's not forget this." With a scrap of silk in his hand, Santos motioned for her to lean forward again. It was a short hood, coming only to the tip of her nose. "This will increase our pleasure and ultimately, yours."

"Yes, master."

She knew they'd moved away when the air turned cooler. A wave of panic washed over her. She couldn't see anything, her hands were tied behind her back and hundreds of people could be staring at her right now.

They will keep me safe...they will keep me safe...

Taking deep, even breaths, the panic began to ease and the

sounds of the party moved into the forefront. The familiar clink of crystal, female laughter and the occasional sound of flesh against flesh reached her ears, reminding her that wasn't alone. She was surrounded by others here to enjoy the same things as she.

"Looks like someone was behaving badly." A male voice sounded to her left. "Just look at that ass. Man I'd like to paddle this one."

"She is lovely," a female voice sounded. "Spread those cheeks and let's see what she's hiding."

Hands touched her buttocks and she bit her lip to keep from screaming. Strong male fingers spread her cheeks to expose her anus. Jane gulped even as a gush of cream trickled from her pussy.

"Look at that beautiful rose." The woman sighed.

"I'll bet she's as tight as a fist too." The man released her. "Gentlemen, you have a treasure in this one."

"We think so." Antonio sounded amused.

The next few minutes were a blur of voices and intimate touches from faceless strangers. At the request of one man, Antonio commanded her to spread her legs. The stranger didn't touch her, but she felt the unmistakable heat of his breath on her inner thighs.

Jane couldn't remember a time when she had felt so edgy. The craving for a release had only increased since Antonio had helped her onto the pedestal and most of the spectators never touched her. Her breasts were engorged and her nipples throbbed with each beat of her heart. Her pussy was so wet the juices had left trails down her thighs. Damn! Was anyone going to give her ease?

"Gentlemen, what do we have here?" A deep, masculine voice jolted her back to reality. "I don't remember meeting this one."

"You haven't. She's quite new to the scene."

Jane caught a slight tension in Antonio's voice. Did they know each other?

"Villareal, you seem to have all the luck. Where do you find them?"

His voice moved around her, telling her the stranger was looking at her from all sides. He stopped in front of her and from beneath the edge of the hood she spied a pair of polished leather boots.

"I see she's been disciplined recently." The man sounded amused. "Are you still training with old school methods?"

"They work the best for us," Santos answered. "She is in the early stages of her training and, as I'm sure you know, reprimanding a submissive is an important part of her schooling."

"How well I know this." The man circled around her again. "I've learned that I enjoy the training phase tremendously, almost more than the finished product. I've trained a great many submissives in the ancient art of service."

His voice sounded close, he must be quite tall.

"Your reputation precedes you," Antonio said. "We are great admirers of your work."

"You flatter me." The boots stopped directly in front of her. "What is her name?"

"*Belleza*, we call her Beauty."

"She certainly is that though her name isn't terribly original, gentlemen." He chuckled. "May I?"

"It would be an honor."

A change in the air currents signaled him moving closer. Her skin prickled.

"*Belleza*, my name is Archer."

"Good evening, Mr. Archer." Her voice was husky.

"Just...Archer." He sounded amused.

A hand touched her leg and she couldn't help but tense.

"Is this her first time?"

"It is," Santos said.

"That explains it." His hand moved up her leg. "The purpose of displaying a submissive is two-fold, Beauty. The first is obvious; to arouse the slave until the pleasure-pain line is blurred. This state of heightened arousal is instrumental in bringing a slave to heel." His fingers stroked the sensitive back of one knee. "The other is to demonstrate the slave's level of submission and the talent of her masters. Yours must think a great deal of you to display you so early in your training."

His hand moved above her knee and without thinking, she shifted her feet to give him better access.

"Greedy one isn't she?"

"That she is." Santos's tone held a note of warning.

"Slave, arch your back and show off those exquisite nipples," Archer commanded.

She did as he asked. The stiff lace trim chafed at her exposed nipples, and she swallowed a whimper. The urge to writhe like a cat in heat was strong. When the stranger's hand touched her pussy she couldn't prevent a strangled squeal from escaping.

"Silence!"

Archer spoke only moments before a hand struck her ass. Need spiraled through her blood and her cream flooded her pussy. Helpless, she bucked against the hand on her mound. Beneath the edge of the hood she could see his hands. They were strong, tanned and the nails were clean and neatly trimmed. On the left he wore a dime-sized ruby ring.

"She's fiery, passionate." His fingers spread her pussy lips. "No piercings? No tattoos? What a rarity you have."

"We think so." Antonio's voice was closer now.

"May I?" Archer spoke.

"Please."

Jane didn't have an opportunity to be nervous. One minute he was spreading her labia and the next, his mouth covered her. Strong hands gripped her ass cheeks, holding her in place, while his tongue began to stroke.

Remaining quiet wasn't an option. A shriek was torn from her and need rose hard and fast. Thrusting her hips forward she tried to force him to increase the pressure on her clit, but he was in control. Another slap to her ass and she backed off.

Just a few strokes of his tongue told her all she needed to know about the stranger. He was well-schooled in the art of eating pussy. A slow, deep suck caused her knees to buckle but somehow he managed to keep her on her feet. Her hips rocked against him, she was close...so close...

"Man, I'd like to fuck that pussy."

The strange voice entered her sensual fog, and she became aware of a growing audience watching them.

"Isn't that Archer?"

"...just look at her tits..."

"...I've heard that man is a maestro when it comes to eating cunt..."

"...watch how she thrusts against his mouth..."

"I'd like to tear that ass up..."

The flow of voices ratcheted her arousal higher, and Jane didn't know how much more she could withstand. Against her will her hips rolled forward, increasing the pressure on her clit. She was so close, just...one...more...

A sharp spank landed across her ass. Shock doused her body like ice water and she screamed. It was a long, sharp sound that rose above the music to echo throughout the room.

"*Belleza*, you forget yourself." Santos's voice was stern. "We did not give you permission to come."

"Yes, master."

Her lips felt numb, and her head was spinning.

"Her taste is exquisite," Archer said. Firm hands landed on her breasts, gently kneading and plumping them before giving each nipple a tug. "And no implants, how utterly delicious."

"One of many reasons she is so special to us."

Antonio's voice sounded at her elbow. Relief washed over her, pushing her need for release down, for now at least.

"Are you amenable to a possible transaction?" Archer sounded bored. "I would make her one of my women."

"Sorry, she's not for auction." Antonio's voice was firm. "Her training has barely begun, and we're looking forward to working with her. Even in such a short period of time, we've grown quite fond of her and we have no intentions of relinquishing our control."

"Villareal, I took you for a smart man." Archer sounded annoyed. "Fondness is a serious handicap when training a slave. The introduction of feelings into the arrangement only serve to create a lazy submissive and her masters...sloppy."

"We can assure you, there's no danger of that." Santos spoke. "Proper training is our first concern."

"I'll pay one million dollars for thirty days with her, alone."

Archer's voice rang out and all conversation died. Even the music seemed to fade into the background. Stunned, Jane wondered if she'd heard right. Did he just offer one million dollars...for her? She'd heard many auction anecdotes but never one that commanded such an outrageous figure.

Slave auctions were more common in the hardcore bondage underground in Europe than here in the states. Masters would sell their slaves, with their permission of course, to a more experienced master for training. Once the fee was paid, the slave was turned over to their new master for a predetermined period of time, usually a few months.

The master and his new slave then undertook an intensive training course in the art of submission. And when the release date arrived, the submissives returned to their original master fully trained and ready for service.

The money was turned over to the submissive. She'd heard of many women using the cash to pay for their college education. She frowned. Surely they wouldn't think she'd be interested in such an arrangement...

"As I've already mentioned, she's not up for auction." Antonio's voice was firm.

"I'll not take no for an answer—"

"Good evening, gentlemen." A voice tinged with a familiar French accent broke in. "Archer, you honor us with your presence this evening."

"Bertrand." Archer sounded bored. "I'm interested in retaining this slave for my services—"

Antonio growled.

"I'm sorry old friend." Jean Jacques' tone was cheerful. "This young woman isn't available for auction. Now if you'd like to accompany me, we have some beautiful—"

"Why would I look at any of them when I have found the one I desire?" The note of obstinacy in Archer's words was unmistakable.

"Out of the question." Jean Jacques was firm. "This slave is a new acquisition and her masters are enamored—"

"Which makes her all the more desirable," Archer drawled. "I seek only the most exclusive women for training."

"She's lovely and while I can understand your disappointment." Jean Jacques' voice dropped a notch. "Her masters will not relinquish her. So let us console ourselves with some of Dirk's finest brandy and a cigar on the terrace."

Archer didn't answer immediately, and the guests seemed to hold their collective breath waiting for his answer. After a few moments, she heard him curse under his breath.

"Only if you insist, Bertrand," Archer muttered. "Villareal, this matter isn't settled between us."

A chill ran down her spin.

"I look forward to the next time we meet, Archer." Antonio's tone was mocking. "But we can assure you, this isn't a challenge you will win no matter the offer."

"Every man, and woman, has a price." He chuckled. "Even you, Spaniard."

The crowd broke out into whispers, and Jane's knees began to shake. She'd never dreamed of entering into an auction, and she was grateful Antonio and Santos had taken care of the situation so efficiently.

"Hold still, *Belleza*," Santos hissed. "We'll get you out of here."

She felt a tug on the scarf binding her wrists and the material slipped away. Strong arms snatched her off the pedestal and the whispers increased in volume. She recognized Antonio's scent, and she threw her arms around his neck.

"You're safe, Jane." His breath was warm on her cheek.

"We've got you."

So the bitch had landed on her feet after all.

Peter Ellington scowled at the swinging door Jane and her keepers had used. A good portion of that money should be his as he had been the one to introduce the woman to bondage play in the first place. God knew he needed the money. Keeping up with his expensive whore and her growing cocaine habit was a serious financial drain. He'd have to get rid of her soon.

He grimaced as he tossed back a shot of tequila. Besides, it was his hand that had first slapped Jane's chunky ass and it was his cock she'd begged for. Slapping the glass down on the bar, he nodded for the bartender to give him a refill.

What a little liar she was.

The last time they'd been together she'd played the victim card. She'd acted so upset over being asked to become his mistress and now, now she'd hooked up with two men determined to fuck the most beautiful pussies in the world. Neither one of them would ever marry the silly cow. Hell, she was older than both of them.

His lip curled.

He really shouldn't be surprised. A woman with her overactive sex drive would hump anything when the mood struck her. The fact she'd latched onto Prentice's half-brother was a shocker. Where they hell had they even crossed paths? Jane didn't socialize in their world. She was the hired help.

He downed the second shot of tequila.

Villareal had a lengthy and vivid reputation when it came to women. His smug face appeared on the covers of tabloid magazines at least once a week with a different bitch on each arm. His decision to bed Jane was perplexing. Why would he want her when he could have Giselle back? God knew she was hot to get him and his sizable wallet back into her hands. Giselle might be cold hearted, but her body was hot enough to keep any man warm.

Jane had been holding out on him. While they were together she hadn't displayed even an ounce of the adventuresome spirit he'd witnessed with Archer. Turning away from the bar, he started toward the door. He'd have to do something to rectify the situation. He hadn't invested all those long hours of training to allow another man to sweep in and take what was rightfully his. He began to smile.

He wasn't a man who liked to lose.

Chapter Five

Jane's mind was spinning when Antonio brought her into the library. Santos followed, pausing only to shut the doors. Pulling off the hood, she stood in Antonio's arms looking from one man to another.

"You are fucking brilliant!" Antonio squeezed her tight.

"Oh no, *amigo*. Our Jane is more than brilliant. She is the stuff of fantasies."

Jane started to laugh, and she snatched her skirt away from Santos. Holding onto Antonio, she wiggled into the garment.

"You're making me blush."

Santos took her arm and pulled her away from Antonio. Without missing a step he swept her into an energetic waltz. Jane clung to his strong arms. She'd yet to see him so carefree, and his wide smile warmed her heart.

"They were disappointed when we stole you away." Antonio twirled her away from Santos. "Many a man will dream of you tonight."

"I really didn't do anything—"

"And everyone will envy us for having the exotic Jane in our bed." Santos stole her away again.

"There isn't anything exotic about me." She was laughing

so hard she was breathless.

"We think there is." Santos gave her a mock leer. "Antonio, I believe we have unfinished business to attend to."

"Business? This late?" The last thing she wanted was to share her men with anyone else.

"Ah, yes, *Belleza*." Santos slowed the dance then dipped her. "You are our business. Your masters are in need of your services."

The gleam in his eyes left her in no doubt what those services might entail. Her pussy throbbed as Santos escorted her to a grand piano. Set on a riser, the instrument was polished to a high finish. Wide windows overlooked the gardens and thousands of fairy lights glowed against the darkness. With the domed glass ceiling above, it felt as if they were outside.

"Do you have any requests?" Antonio ran his fingers over the keys.

"Maestro, play something...stormy."

"Carmina Burana it is then."

Santos's swept her off her feet and placed her on the piano. When Antonio began to play, the notes worked their way up her spine to vibrate throughout her body. Pleasure curled in her belly.

"This is lovely." She sighed with pleasure.

Santos laid his hands on her knees and there was no mistaking his desire. Reaching for him, she slid her hands around his neck.

"Outside, they will see us." She nodded toward the window.

"Do you care?" His smile was wicked.

"Not in the slightest." She answered his smile with a soft kiss. "I am Beauty, a woman to be pleasured."

"That you are." His hands slid down her thighs. "And now

you have a job to do. I'd like you to accompany our friend."

Pulling her toward him, he spread her thighs leaving Jane no choice but to lie back. At the first touch of his tongue, she arched. A wail was torn from her as each silken stroke of his tongue sent shockwaves through her body.

Raising her arms over her head, she latched onto the edge of the piano. Sparks burst against her eyelids, and she thrust upward forcing her clit harder against his tongue. The tempo of the music increased as did her cries. The loudest came when Santos stopped and eased her legs from his shoulders.

"I never said you could come, did I, slave?" His smile was wicked.

"No, master." Her voice was a mere whimper.

"Move backward and assume the position."

Sluggishly, Jane inched back to the center of the piano thankful for her velvet skirt as it allowed her to slide with little effort. Turning her over, Santos joined her, helping her to her knees. There wasn't a lot of room so she crossed her arms and rested her forehead on them.

"Excellent."

When he spread her cheeks, she winced. She was still sensitive from her earlier discipline.

"Tonight you've pleased me very much, *Belleza.*" Santos pressed a finger firmly against her anus. "We've drawn a crowd outside, and I think we should give them a show."

Jane glanced out the windows and saw he was right. A small group of costumed guests was gathered on the paths openly staring at them.

"Would you like that, my slave?" he crooned. "Me fucking you in the ass while our friends watch us?"

"Yes, master," she whispered.

He applied gel to her anus, taking care to ensure she was properly prepared. The stroke of his fingers was both soothing and arousing. The caress stopped. She heard the metallic whisk of a zipper and then felt the broad head of his cock press against her.

She moaned, pushing her hips toward him.

"Patience," he sounded strained.

Increasing the pressure, he slipped past the right ring of muscle and worked himself inside inch by delicious inch. When he began to thrust, she met him stroke for stroke. Animal-like sounds emerged from his throat and the slap of his balls against her flesh was felt more than heard. When he touched her clit, she knew it was over.

Her orgasm was immediate and violent. The room swirled around her as wave after wave of pummeled her flesh and held her in its thrall. The music crashed around her drenching her in shafts of colored light. Santos continued stroking her clit with his slick finger and a second release came hard on the heels of the first. She was floating, soaring...

His grip on her hips tightened when he came. His body jerked once, twice, three times before coming to a rest. After a few moments he withdrew leaving her empty, needy. Even though she'd had two mind-blowing orgasms, her hunger persisted. She craved another then another and another...

Strong hands rolled her over onto her back. Forcing open her eyes, she saw it was Antonio who leaned over her. Sweat gleamed on his upper lip and he was struggling to free his engorged cock from his pants. Beneath her, the piano came to life.

Mmm... It would seem he'd enjoyed the show.

Mustering what little strength remained, she sat up. Reaching for him, she touched his cock then leaned forward to taste him. Swirling her tongue over the broad head, his hips thrust forward. Silk over steel, she stroked his erection tasting the salt of his need.

"*Belleza*, stop."

His words barely registered before he pulled his cock from her mouth. Spreading her legs wide, he entered her with a powerful thrust, and she was sobbing with gratitude. Antonio was a big man both horizontally and vertically, and she was going to take advantage of every delicious inch.

"You're fucking beautiful," he panted. "Watching Santos fuck you in the ass was delicious misery."

Desire burned her from the inside out as a warm shivery chasm burst open in her lower belly. Antonio gathered her close and their lips met in a kiss so carnal, so animal that she burned. Greedy hands gripped, teased and caressed as their bodies surged and lunged in the battle for supremacy.

Again and again her body took its pleasure, clenching around his cock as sheer bliss poured through her body like melted chocolate, filling all of the empty nooks and crannies in her soul. Spasms washed over her like raindrops, each one sharper and more complex than the one before.

Antonio's face contorted, and his hips lost their rhythm. Tightening her thighs around his hips, he threw back his head, the muscles in his neck stood in sharp relief as he came. His mouth was open, but she heard no sound, only the pounding of the music. He was so beautiful, so raw.

When he began to come down she wrapped her arms around him, savoring the sensation of his body over hers. She began to smile. What a difference a day made. She'd come here looking to get laid, instead she'd found two men who threatened to steal her heart.

"Saint Anthony, Saint Anthony, please come around. Something is lost and cannot be found...mainly my mind."

Lily was so nervous her body was vibrating like a tuning fork. Jean Jacques would be here any minute and all she could do was pace. Her stomach twisted.

What the hell are you thinking, girl?

That was a good question, too bad she didn't have an answer. The madness that had overtaken her in the ballroom was gone, leaving a cold, hard pit in her stomach. Why had she allowed Robert to talk her into this?

Jean Jacques hurt you...

So what else is new? Her lips twisted. It wasn't as if he were the first to wound her pride.

But this time your heart was involved.

Therein lay the crux of the issue. Jean Jacques had called her a tease then demanded she submit to him. When she refused, he'd screwed another woman in the same room where they'd made love the first time. Images flashed through her mind. Rachel Van de Kemp on her knees with his cock in her mouth...Jean Jacques' beautiful hands on another woman's body.

This was why she was going to fuck Robert on the pool table. Jean Jacques would see them, and he'd hurt as much as she did. Childish? Yes, but this time she was determined to have the upper hand.

"You're so deep in thought a marching band could come through here and you'd never notice."

Lily scowled at Robert when he strolled through the door. With a Scotch in one hand and a lazy smile on his face, he looked as if he didn't have a worry in his head. Then again, what did he have to be concerned about? His heart wasn't involved, and he was about to get laid with barely lifting a finger.

"You scared me," she hissed.

"Then maybe you should pay attention to what is going on around you." Leaving his glass on a table, Robert removed his jacket. "Jean Jacques was still talking to Archer when I left so we have a few minutes."

"Good. Good."

When she passed the entrance, she glanced down the long tiled hallway. With the door propped open, Jean Jacques would see them when he turned the corner. The best part was, they'd see him too.

What if he didn't show? Or worse yet, what if he wasn't alone? Her cheeks burned. Humiliating the man she loved wasn't part of the plan. He would forgive her for many things, but his pride was as hard and high as hers. Humiliating him was a wound that may never be healed.

"You're beautiful when you're worried."

Robert stood next to the pool table watching her. His shirt was crumpled on the floor along with his belt. The top button of his pants was undone and the zipper was halfway down. He'd always been in excellent physical condition, but now he looked bigger, more tanned.

"Then again you were always beautiful," he said.

"I can't take credit for good genes." She gestured to his well-defined abs. "Europe has been good for you."

"It was the nude beaches. There was no way I was going to drop my drawers and be chased off by crowds of traumatized sun bathers."

"You were always hot, and you know it." When Lily placed her hand on his hard stomach, his muscles flexed beneath his skin.

"Lily, are you flirting with me?" He covered her hand with his.

"Don't I always?"

"And you do it well."

Dropping his hand, he unzipped his pants. Robert certainly wasn't lying about the nude beaches as there wasn't a tan line to be seen. She blinked. Well, there could be tan lines, but she'd never notice because the sight of his cock caused her concentration to fly from her mind.

Jutting from a nest of dark hair, his member was growing longer and thicker before her gaze. He was the only man she'd ever been with who was ready for sex every minute of the day or night. He seemed to be in a semi-aroused state all the time.

"I only ask—" his voice grew husky, "—because I can assure you, I'm a sure thing."

"Robert, you were always a sure thing," she teased.

Taking her hand, he brought it down to his groin. Her fingers curled around his rigid length, and he captured her shoulders. Their lips met and his grip tightened, pressing his body against hers.

She'd forgotten what a skilled kisser he was. Nipping, sucking, licking, he was everywhere at once, dissolving her anxiety and arousing her body. A wave of heat struck, shafted through her body and she moaned. His hips thrust forward, forcing his cock through her fingers.

The last thing she'd expected was pleasure. Their coming together was about punishment, not release. They were here to teach Jean Jacques a lesson...but her body had stopped listening when his mouth touched hers. Surrounded by his familiar taste, his scent, Lily responded on a primal level.

Revenge was forgotten as the need to mate surged forth. Animal-like moans worked their way up her throat and the desire to throw him down and take him was strong.

His fingers dug into her thighs as he pulled up her skirt. She groaned when he palmed her ass, his big hands flexing and releasing in a pulse not unlike the sex act. Tightening her grip on his cock, she began to stroke. His moan sent a jolt of liquid need to her pussy. Her nipples ached and she rubbed her breasts against him.

The slap of flesh on flesh and a sting on her ass jerked her from the sensual haze they'd created. He'd spanked her again!

"Damn you, Robert."

Before she could complete the thought, he'd bent her over the pool table. Flipping up her skirt, he forced her legs apart then pinned her hips to the table with his body. His cock ground against her sex and the resulting rush of pleasure obliterated her annoyance.

Besides, revenge was a dish best served cold.

"You want it bad don't you, baby?" Rolling his hips, he slammed his cock against her cunt. "Your pussy is begging for it."

His rough language was both a shock and a turn on. This was new territory for them and while it had thrown her off, she wasn't about to back down from a challenge.

"Fuck, yeah I do, stud." She squirmed against his erection. "You'd better be man enough to deliver."

"Hang on, bitch. I'm going to take you on the ride of your life."

Lily pressed backward as he thrust forward. The broad head of his cock slammed into her cunt. His fingers dug into her hips and a cat-like scream was torn from her. Arching her back, she used her arms like shock absorbers to propel her backward when he lunged into her. Heat threatened to devour her and the sound of slapping flesh punctuated with moans and cries rebounded off the walls.

Taking her by the shoulders, Robert pulled her upright until his chest met her back. Gripping her blouse in one hand, he shredded the cloth with a single jerk.

"You like it rough don't you, Lily?" He captured a nipple and rolled it between his fingers. "A little pain with your pleasure? Well, I'm happy to oblige."

Heat mixed with pain seared her flesh. Her breath caught when she saw something moving in the hallway out of the corner of her eye.

It was Jean Jacques.

A wave of ice cascaded over her. He was watching them and judging his tight expression, he wasn't terribly pleased with her. Then again, she wasn't happy with him either.

Borrowing a move from a porn movie, she tilted her chin then licked her lips. Cupping her breasts, she stuck out her tongue to lick her own nipple.

"What a gorgeous little fuck doll you are, Lily," Robert moaned. "I could screw you all day and come back the next."

Jean Jacques' lips pulled back from his teeth in a snarl so fierce her stomach dropped. Reaching for his pants, his movements were uncoordinated as he fumbled with the zipper. When he managed to get it down, his hand plunged into his pants to unleash his cock.

The bastard was enjoying this.

Raising his hand, he licked the palm before wrapping it around his erect cock. Her eyes widened when he started to masturbate. Any pretense of grace was gone as he worked his hand over his cock like a horny schoolboy. With Robert's cock fucking her like a freight train and Jean Jacques yanking at his with a vengeance, she didn't think she could get any more aroused.

Shivers took hold of her body. Even though she'd gone into this with the idea of faking her pleasure, the need for falsehoods was long past.

"Harder," she moaned. "Fuck me harder."

Robert's thrusts had deteriorated to the level of a caveman's. His fingers bruised her hips and his balls slapped at the lower curve of her buttocks.

"A man would be insane to let you get away." His voice was distorted, breathless. "If you were mine, I'd fuck you so often you'd think of no one but me."

Lily caught the flash of pain in Jean Jacques eyes. His nostrils flared and his skin had taken on a slight sheen of sweat. His cheeks were flushed and a mixture of rage and desire waged war on his face.

Sliding her hand over the curve of her belly, she slipped her fingers into her pussy. With each stroke of Jean Jacques' hand on his cock, she slid her fingers over her slippery clit. She was on fire from the inside out.

"I need to come, please," she panted. "I'm yours, yours, yours, yours..."

Robert pushed her down on the table forcing her to break eye contact with Jean Jacques.

"No—"

Her protest was cut short when felt Robert spread her ass cheeks. Sucking in a noisy breath, she squealed when he pressed a finger against the tight ring of her anus.

"Oh Godddd..."

Thrusting his finger home, her eyes rolled back in her head. Her need for release tore through her body leaving her powerless in the face of the storm. Her cunt pulsed around his cock, and she screamed. Spots swirled against her eyelids and her body pulsed with each delicious spasm. Drained, she allowed her forehead to come to a rest on the table.

Robert came hard, the jerking of his cock seemed to last for hours. If she'd had the energy, she might have managed to come again. Instead she remained limp, shivering through the waves of his release.

After a few long moments she managed to pull herself together enough to raise her head. Jean Jacques was gone.

"I will keel the beech," Giselle snapped.

"Shut up." Annoyed, Peter shoved her into an empty bathroom. "We don't want anyone to hear us."

"Bah, zey won't pay attention." She waved her hand in the air. "Zey know I am ver-we passionate."

"Well passionate or not, we don't need anyone to hear us." He locked the door.

"Whoever zhe blonde beech is, I make her disappear like zhat." She snapped her fingers.

"Where did they meet?"

"I doan know."

"How long has she been with them?"

"'Ow would I know?" She flopped down on a chair in front of the mirror. "Tony 'ad to 'ave peeked up zee whore 'ere in Denverre."

Peter scowled. He'd been trying to set up a meeting with both Villareal and Santos, but they'd been in and out of the country several times in the past few months and their schedules had yet to coincide. So how had Jane managed an introduction while he couldn't even get a return call...

They met this weekend.

His fist clenched. Jane, for all of her bottomless libido, wasn't exactly free with her favors. Yes, they'd had sex the night they met, but she'd kept him at arm length for the next three weeks.

"What a fucking tease," he growled.

"I zee zhat look on your faze. What are you planning?" Giselle turned toward him. "And 'ow can I help?"

"I'd like to know more about the slave auctions."

Jane and Santos were sitting in a quiet corner of the gardens, away from the lights and wandering guests. After dinner, Dirk had stolen away with Antonio leaving them to wander the grounds by themselves.

"How familiar are you with the auction process?" Santos slid his arm around her shoulders.

"I'm not." Making a mental note to burn them, Jane kicked off her shoes. "Peter explained the basics to me. Potential submissives enter into an arrangement with a master to be trained. Is it like a boot camp for bondage?"

"Close enough." Santos stretched out his long legs. "Have you ever heard the name, Archer Drengr?"

"No. Is that the man from the ballroom?" A faint breeze caressed her cheeks. "Am I correct to assume from your conversation that he's a trainer?"

"He's not just any master. He's notorious on the continent, and his services are highly sought after. Any submissive trained by Archer will command top dollar for his or her services."

"Isn't that prostitution?" Jane wrinkled her nose.

"Americans." He shot her an amused look. "Contrary to what you believe, bondage isn't about the physical release. The most important component is strictly psychological. In order to seduce the body, one must begin with the mind.

"Archer's students are trained to submit both mentally and physically. Their capitulation is so deeply ingrained into their psyche that it is said they are capable of reaching levels of pleasure most can only dream about."

"What do you mean?"

"They achieve orgasm strictly through the bondage process without sexual stimulation. Their arousal is derived from the act of submission."

"So they are turned on by serving their master?"

"It's more complicated than that but yes, you're on the right track."

"Wow." She snuggled deeper into his side. "But, doesn't that make them, well, passive in life?"

"You would think so but no, that doesn't seem to be the case. Some of his earliest slaves have moved on to conquer their chosen professions. To outsiders the common assumption is submissives have passive tendencies when the opposite is usually true. The vast majority of sexual submissives are goal-oriented, so much so that they desire giving up control sexually as a means of bringing balance into their lives."

"So they give up control of themselves as a way of equalizing the weight of their professions? Multi-millionaire by day, submissive by night."

"Don't let Dirk hear you make that analogy," he teased. "Archer has a discerning eye and it's considered a major coup that he approached you."

"I know I should be flattered but I have to admit, he

creeped me out a little." Feeling foolish, she ducked her head.

"He's a strong personality, and he's used to getting his way. When he sees what he wants, he takes it." His arm tightened. "It's a good trait to have in a master."

"Yeah, but..." she shook her head, "...there was something about him that made me uneasy. It was almost as if he knew what was going on in my head before I did."

"*Belleza*, you have nothing to fear." He kissed her temple. "He appreciates beautiful women and he's dedicated to his craft, but he's not a madman."

"News flash, serial killers look just like your next door neighbor." She laid her head on his shoulder.

"What an imagination you have." He chuckled. "I've come to know several of his students, and they have nothing but praise for him."

"That may be, but I think I'll pass."

"Good. Antonio and I don't like to share our toys." He laid his cheek against her hair. "Other than your experience with Archer, what did you think of being displayed?"

What did she think about an experience that made her feel like the most beautiful woman in the world?

"It was powerful. Terrifying, thrilling and I never wanted it to stop."

"So you'd like to do it again?"

"Hell yes."

"Excellent. You were the most exquisite woman in the room. When Archer was licking you, I thought Antonio was going to come out of his skin."

"Only Antonio?"

"Are you fishing for compliments?" He was laughing. "Everyone in that room wanted to be inside you, myself included."

"Is that so?" Jane laid her hand on this hard thigh. "And, now? Do you want to be inside me?"

"How can you even ask?" His voice dropped to a growl. "I've been hard since you came out of the bathroom in your costume."

Jane wiggled out of his embrace then rose, wincing when the gravel dug into her tender feet. Straddling his legs, she climbed onto his lap. Wrapping her arms around his neck, she snuggled close. His rock-hard body radiated heat and strength, and she could use a little of both.

Her gaze moved over his beautiful face. Deep brown eyes that were usually so hard, guarded were open, trusting. A slight smile played at the corners of his mouth, and she couldn't resist pressing her lips to his. They were soft, gentle against hers. Her tongue slipped out to lick at the seam of his mouth. His tongue met hers and all gentleness dissolved away.

She moaned when he sucked her tongue. His teeth tugged on her lower lip, and she squirmed closer. Her fingers tangled in his hair and her hips began to move. He groaned as if he were wounded when she pressed against his erection.

His hands landed on her thighs, and he pushed her skirt up. When he moved his hand between her thighs, his mouth muffled her sigh. His fingers slipped into her pussy, and she thrust against his hand.

"You're so wet, so sweet," he spoke against her lips. "Fuck, Jane. If I don't get inside you soon I'm going to lose it."

"Hurry, please."

He reached for his zipper, but Jane stopped him.

"Let me."

It took some interesting gyrations but finally she managed

to free him. He groaned when she took him in her hand.

"I want you to scream for me, *Belleza*." His hands latched onto her waist. "Let everyone hear how I make you feel—"

A soft beep interrupted him, and he cursed.

"What was that?"

Putting a hand to his ear, he muttered something in Spanish. His expression turned dark and his body tensed beneath her. Whatever was going on, it didn't appear to be good news.

"I'm outside, and I'll be there in a minute." He dropped his hand.

"What's going on? Is something wrong?"

"There is something I need to take care of, but it's nothing you need to worry about."

"Are you sure?" She scrambled off his lap.

"Yes, I'm sure." He struggled to stuff his erection back into his pants. "Let me walk you back to the house."

"I'd rather stay out here if you don't mind." She nodded toward the crowded terrace. "It's so nice and peaceful out here and I don't feel like facing the madness quite yet."

"I'm not sure that's such a good idea." His sharp gaze scanned the area.

"Just give me ten minutes. I'll be in shortly." She smiled up at him.

"And you promise me you won't leave this area?" He seemed distracted, his mind already on whatever task awaited him.

"I won't." She lifted her foot and wiggled her bare toes. "See, no shoes."

"I see that." He kissed her cheek. "If I don't see you inside in the next ten minutes, I'm coming to find you."

He walked away, his long stride covered the distance to the house much faster than when they'd walked out. Then again, he wasn't wearing the most ridiculous shoes in the world.

Taking a deep breath, Jane exhaled slowly. She hadn't lied about needing a few minutes alone. The events of the past day and half were catching up to her, and she was beginning to wind down. Tired or not, she didn't regret a second of it. She'd met two amazing men who'd not only fulfilled her dreams, but they'd far exceeded them. Few women would ever be able to indulge in absolute decadence as she had this weekend.

It's almost over...

In the morning it would be over and what then? Would it be too bold if she asked them to continue the relationship? Would they want to?

She sighed. What was the proper etiquette for a situation such as this? She would bet Ms. Manners had never faced a situation as difficult as this-

"Hello, Jane."

Startled, she looked up. A strange man dressed as Henry the Eighth stood in front of her. With a mask covering most of his face, she didn't recognize him immediately, but the voice was vaguely familiar.

"I'm sorry, do I know you?"

"I'm not surprised you'd forget me so soon, not with two men to keep you satisfied."

Her eyes widened when he removed the mask. It was Peter.

"Maybe it has nothing to do with them." Squinting, she scanned the ground looking for her shoes. "It could be that you weren't terribly memorable."

"You always had a smart mouth." He laughed. "It will be my

pleasure to curb you of that tendency."

"Peter, you can't do a damned thing where I'm concerned." Locating one shoe, she snatched it up. Where the hell was the other one?

"That's where you're wrong."

A metallic click sounded, and Jane froze.

Chapter Six

"The first time I saw you I thought you were the most beautiful creature I'd ever seen."

Lily started when Jean Jacques' voice intruded upon her moping. After leaving Robert she'd snuck up to the third floor to grab a few minutes alone. Only the few minutes had stretched into hours and she felt no better now than when she'd sat down.

Crushing a tear-stained tissue in her fist, she turned. He stood in the center of the solarium less than ten feet away. His shoes were gone, and his clothing looked as if he'd been rolling on the floor. His hair stood on end as if he'd been running his fingers through it. Even disheveled and unhappy, he was still the most handsome man she'd ever seen.

"You wore a white dress with yellow trim, a giant hat with flowers and a pair of heels so high I didn't see how you could walk." His smile was sad. "While you're not very big you threw me for a loop."

"I remember that outfit. It was Kitten's first garden party, and all the ladies wore hats." She frowned. "But I don't remember you being there."

"You never saw me." He shrugged. "I watched you all afternoon from this very window. Even in those shoes you still ran from one end of the grounds to the other, and you didn't fall once."

She laughed though her eyes started to sting.

"I think I fell in love with you that day." He looked away. "And it's been torture ever since."

A tear slid down her cheek.

"I fell in love with you when I was a child, well, the idea of you." Lily turned to stare unseeingly out the windows. "I would dream of a handsome prince who would see me from across a room and fall in love with me. We'd steal away to his ancestral home and his family would welcome me like one of their own. On the eve of our wedding we'd learn I was the kidnapped daughter of a foreign king and royal in my own right."

"What happened then?"

"We'd be deliriously happy every day of our lives." She laid her hand against the glass. Lights in the garden danced as tears blurred her vision. "I spent hours dreaming up the names of our children."

"That's a wonderful dream." His voice was husky. "Do you think it could still come true?"

"No, but it was a good dream for as long as it lasted." Turning away from the window, she shrugged. "When I hit puberty and realized I'd inherited my mother's ass and she had her mother's ass, there was no mistaking that I was a Tyler."

"And you no longer believe in dreams?"

"Not for me. I'm firmly rooted in the reality of my everyday life."

"Well, I still believe dreams can come true."

Their gazes met, and she saw her sadness reflected in his eyes. Lily had no doubt he saw the same in hers. Pain lanced her heart.

"This was a mistake, Jean Jacques. You and I, together?

We were doomed from the start."

Even as the words were said, she wanted to snatch them back. Their pride had created a chasm, which she didn't have any idea how to heal. Jean Jacques was a man used to leading others, and her mother always accused her of being too independent for her own good.

Their lives together would be nothing but power struggles and heartache, a situation she'd already lived through. Her parents had loved and fought their way through eighteen years of marriage and by the time they had separated they were shells of the people they once were.

"You little liar." He began to laugh. "I can't believe you said that without choking."

"Am not." She scowled at him. "I'm telling you it won't work."

"After two years of intense foreplay and one night of the most amazing lovemaking ever, you are going to walk away as if nothing happened? You are such a fraud."

"I'm calling it quits before we eviscerate each other." Lily was practically shouting to be heard over his laughter. "I watched my parents tear each other apart until there was nothing left of the person they'd fallen in love with."

"Your parents were fools." He wiped the tears from his eyes. "Melding our lives together could be the adventure of a lifetime."

"Adventure?" Tears were running down her face, but she didn't care. She was so angry with him she could strangle him. "You call thousands of nights hiding under the covers as they screamed at one another a fucking adventure?"

"That should've never been allowed to happen." The sadness was gone from his face and determination had taken its place. "But if you think I'm going to let you use that as an excuse to walk away, you'd better think again."

"Jean Jacques—"

"We're going to have children, loads of them." Removing his jacket, he dropped it on the floor. "And when we're not fighting, fucking or raising our offspring, we'll be stupidly happy splitting our time between my family home in Provence and our home here in Denver."

She shook her head. "You haven't been listening to me. I can't do this."

"I have been listening to you." His tie hit the floor. "I've been listening to you for two long years and now I'm done listening."

"You're kidding." Lily backed away. "This can't be happening."

She'd spent the last two hours wrestling with the decision to submit to him or tell him to piss off. She'd made her decision and said her piece, and he was going to ignore her wishes and take what he wanted.

"Trust me, Lily." He unbuttoned his shirt. "There is nothing remotely amusing about my intentions toward you."

"I've told you that this—" she gestured between them, "—cannot happen again."

"You're lying to yourself." His cufflinks hit the floor then skittered away. "Your pride dictates that you reject me, but your heart doesn't agree."

"You don't know the first thing—"

"An astute man listens with his heart, not his ears. I hear more than the words you speak."

His shirt floated to the floor, and her mind went blank. Memories of kissing every inch of his chest stole the liquid from her mouth.

"Take off your skirt." He reached for his zipper.

"No, Jean Jacques." Her voice was little more than a whisper.

"Never mind." His pants sagged then slid down. He kicked them to the side. "I can tear it off with my teeth."

Her knees went weak.

"Who was that guy fucking you in the game room?" He reached for his boxers. "Was that Armand?"

"Who was the woman you fucked in the closet?" She shot back.

"You know who she is." His boxers pooled around his ankles, and he stepped out of them. "Did you notice her pearls? She has some unusual talents involving very expensive jewelry."

"Is that so? Well Robert has some interesting talents as well." Her back hit the wall.

"Watching that bastard fuck you was one of the hottest things I've ever seen." His eyes glittered. "Am I correct in assuming that little adventure was for me?" He loomed over her, crowding her with his size. Their lips were so close his breath licked at her mouth.

"It was." She was breathless. "I wanted to punish you for screwing—"

"I saw you, Lily." His fists slammed into the wall on either side of her head, and she flinched. "I saw you masturbating while I screwed Ms. Junior League. You were turned on and that pisses you off."

"I only enjoyed it until I realized it was you." Her voice was a mere whisper. "Then I was hurt."

"You accused me of screwing around on you." He grabbed her wrists and yanked them over her head. "I have always and will always be an honorable man. My word is my bond."

The pain on his face tore at her heart. What had she done?

"Jean Jacques—"

"The one thing I always counted on was your trust. I'd done nothing to abuse that trust and still you accused me of screwing another woman. I didn't deserve that and you know it." His thumb touched her lower lip. "I'm not your father, Lily, and I'm not like other men. I don't use women and toss them aside. When you gave yourself to me I understand what a gift you are and in turn I gave myself to you."

She was shaking. His gaze scorched her flesh.

"I am your man."

He took possession of her mouth and everything else flew out of her mind. She longed to sink into him, body and soul.

The sound of tearing cloth didn't faze her. When the hairs of his chest grated against her nipples, she moaned into his mouth. She tried to free her hands, but he was having none of it. She felt a jerk on the waistband of her skirt then it too was gone.

Lifting one leg, she wrapped it around one of his trying desperately to get closer. He released her wrists then lifted her into his arms. Twining her legs around his waist, her fingers tangled in his hair. She didn't know where he was taking her, and she didn't care. As long as he came with her she'd be okay.

The world swooped, and he laid her on a chaise lounge. Covering her, he touched her labia, sending a bolt of fire down her spine.

"Jean Jacques, please." Her grip on his hair tightened. "Come inside me."

His cock probed her pussy before sliding home. In unison they groaned. The sensation of him inside her, filling and stretching her most intimate flesh, was both exhilarating and humbling.

"You're crying." He laid his hand on her cheek.

"So are you." Lily smiled. "Take me home, my prince."

Grabbing her by the waist, he rolled until she was on top. Her breath rushed from her lungs when his cock slammed her clit.

"Show me the way, princess," he hissed.

Rising onto her knees, she began to move. Bracing her hands on his shoulders, she swiveled her hips before sliding down again. Repeating the movement, she leaned forward and licked his flat nipples. Taking one into her mouth, she sucked on the hard little nub before worrying it with her teeth.

"Fuck, woman."

He began to buck, his cock thrusting in and out so hard all she could do was hang on. Her orgasm tore through her, and she screamed and the sound echoed off the walls.

He came with a growl, his hand dug into her flesh as his come was jettisoned into her pussy. Slowly she sank onto him, her breath raging in her lungs. Their bodies covered in sweat, they melted together and she was unable to tell where she ended and he began. His heart thudded in her ear, and she closed her eyes.

It was official. She didn't know what the future held but, she realized one thing, she and Jean Jacques would tear each other apart all right, with lust.

Antonio whipped his shirt off and tossed it into the hamper. A drunken party guest had bumped into him and spilled Scotch on his shirt. Grabbing a washcloth, he turned on the water then lathered to remove the stench of alcohol from his arm.

If it wasn't for this unplanned trip to the suite, he'd be with Jane and Santos in the gardens settling down to enjoy the fireworks. He glanced at his watch. If he hurried, he just might make it.

"*Cher* Antonio, 'ave you missed me?"

He was startled when Giselle walked into his bathroom as if she owned the place. Dressed in a think silk shift, she might as well have been naked. Every bump and curve was visible, and he wondered why she even bothered to dress at all.

"What the hell are you doing here?" He tossed the cloth into the hamper then reached for a towel.

"I'm 'ere to see you. I've missed you."

Her lower lip stuck out in a practiced pout that used to get him every time. Now he only felt mildly annoyed.

"What's the matter, Giselle, Ellington not doing it for you?"

Surprise flashed in her eyes, but she recovered quickly.

"'E's not my luv-air." She propped her hip on the vanity. "But I zee you are keeping an eye on me."

"Not for the reasons you're thinking."

Dropping the towel he started to walk around her, and she moved to intercept. When she molded her body to his all he could do was grimace. Giselle was rabid about every bite she put into her mouth and she spent countless hours working out each day. She'd been nipped, tucked and sucked into the perfect model's silhouette. Pert breasts, tight stomach, a firm ass and legs that went from her neck to the floor.

But she didn't hold a candle to Jane.

Taking her firmly by the arms, he set her away from him.

"You're not welcome here, Giselle." He headed for the closet. "This is my brother's home and while they are the ideal hosts who would never dare to embarrass a guest, I have no such compunctions. Get out of my room before I throw you out."

"Antonio. 'Ow you speek to me." She drifted toward him. Her movements were slow and sexy, designed to send a man's brain straight to his groin.

"Trust me, you deserve worse. You've abused my bank account, gone out of your way to try to embarrass me in the media and now you've come into my brother's home to cause trouble." He pulled a black T-shirt over his head. "My patience with you is at an end."

"I 'ope you treet your beech better zan zis." Her expression turned cold, hard. "What iz 'er name? Jean?"

"Jane, and how I treat her is none of your business." He ground out.

"Why are you wif zis fat beech anyway?"

His arm shot out, and he slapped his hand over her mouth. Pushing her backward, he crowded her against the wall. Her eyes bulged.

"You're not permitted to speak her name, Giselle. She is more of a lady than you could ever hope to become." His face was so close to hers he could smell her fear.

"You will leave this house within the next ten minutes, and you will do so quietly. If you fail to do as I've asked, Santos will be happy to escort you from the grounds." His eyes narrowed. "Do you understand me?"

Her nostrils flared and terror was reflected in her eyes when Santos's name was spoken. Antonio didn't know why she was so afraid of his friend, but he would use whatever weapons he had to get her as far away from Jane as possible.

"Good. For once we have an agreement."

He stalked toward the door and threw it open. Giselle stared at him with such hatred he had to wonder why she wanted him back so much. Pushing her shoulders back, she walked past him. Down the hall he heard the grandfather clock strike one and outside, the first firework exploded.

"You sorry bastard." Her voice was sharp, and her body vibrated with anger. "'E already 'as 'er and you won't want 'er in your bed when 'e's done."

"What are you talking about?" Pulling the door shut, he locked it.

"You're blonde beech." She was walking backward away from him slowly. "You're precious whore is with 'im and you'll nev-air zee 'er again." Her cheeks were flushed, and she began to laugh.

Antonio didn't have to ask who she referred to, he already knew. His skin turned cold, and his blood to ice water.

"Where is she, Giselle? Where did he take her?"

"I doan know, and I doan care. As long as you can't 'ave 'er zen I am—"

Later he wouldn't remember moving toward her. One minute they were in the hallway and the next he had shoved her back against the wall. His hands were around her throat, and her expression went from merriment to abject fear.

"If he hurts a single hair on her head, I will destroy him." His grip tightened. "And once I am done with Ellington, I will hunt you down like a rabid dog and I won't stop until the ground beneath you runs red with your blood."

Her nails dug into his hands and her eyes were wild with fear. It would take less than three minutes to kill her.

"*¡Amigo!*"

Santos's shout jerked Antonio back to reality. His friend and a handful of black-garbed security guards were jogging toward him.

"They saved your life, Giselle. This time."

Slowly he forced his hands to relax before letting go entirely. Giselle slumped to the floor and began to cry.

"She said Ellington has Jane." His gaze met Santos's. "He's taking her off the grounds."

"No, that can't be. I just left her in the gardens only minutes ago."

Another firework detonated and they both looked toward the windows. Everyone was outside watching the show and with the explosions coming so close together no one would hear a woman scream.

Gravel dug into her feet and Jane didn't have to pretend to stumble this time. Sharp rocks dug into her knees, and she cried out. They were in the parking area and no one was around to help. It didn't matter how loud she screamed, the fireworks drowned her out.

"Get up you stupid cow." Peter's fingers dug into her hair, and he yanked her to her feet. "Why do you keep falling?"

"I don't have any shoes on, you asshole."

Tears stung her eyes, and her scalp was throbbing. Had it been ten minutes yet? It seemed like hours had passed since Santos had left her side.

"What the fuck did you do with your shoes?"

He began walking again, this time towing her behind him using her hair like a leash.

"They were hurting, and I took them off. I was trying to get them when you shoved that damned gun in my face."

"I'll bet you're regretting that decision now." He chuckled.

"I'm regretting quite a few of my recent decisions," she muttered. "You can't just drive out of here with me in your car, the guards will stop you."

"They'd have to see you first." A metallic click sounded and the trunk of a sleek black Cadillac popped open. "Trust me, they won't even know you're in the car. Get in."

Aghast, she stared at the open compartment. She'd always had a touch of claustrophobia. Consequently she'd go out of her way to avoid any kind of confined space.

Climbing into a car trunk was definitely high on the list of things not to do.

"No, I can't."

She started to back away when he yanked her back. Her sore knees slammed into the bumper and pain tore through her legs. Panic threatened to overwhelm her, and she began to fight.

Screaming at the top of her lungs, she ignored the pain as she thrashed against him. Twisting and turning, she struggled to break his grip. Her bare feet did little damage to his shins, but that didn't stop her.

"Don't make me hurt you, Jane."

She brought up her knee, but he deflected the movement. His fist slammed into the side of her head, and she staggered. Spots danced in front of her eyes, and she barely felt him shove her backward into the trunk. The last thing she saw was his triumphant expression before the lid slammed shut.

Across the parking lot Santos saw Ellington strike Jane. She staggered and her hands came up as if she were trying to protect herself. Ellington shoved her backward, and she fell into the trunk.

He began to run. With every step the veneer of a cultured gentleman dissolved and the boy who'd struggled to survive emerged. Ignoring the men following him, he was focused on his prey. Everything else faded away leaving only the sound of his heartbeat in his ears.

A low growl emerged from his throat and increased in volume with every stride. Startled, Ellington swung toward him, and Santos caught sight of the gun in his hand. The other man raised his arm and shouted something, but Santos didn't slow his gait. He was so close...

Leaping, he was airborne when he saw the flash of light from the weapon. Something struck him, tearing through his upper arm. It burned like fire, but the pain was secondary to his need for vengeance. No one terrorized his woman and lived.

He slammed into the other man so hard Ellington was knocked off his feet and the gun flew out of his hand. Landing on the gravel with a jarring crunch, Santos rolled automatically. Slamming the other man's head into the gravel, he was surprised when Ellington flipped him in a simple college wrestling move. He was pinned under a man who outweighed him by fifty pounds.

But college wrestling was no match for a man who'd survived some of the harshest streets in the world.

Twisting, Santos grabbed him by the throat and thrust backward. Bringing up his leg, he struck Ellington in the back of his head with his shin. Stunned, the lawyer's grip slipped, and Santos flipped him backward.

Sitting astride the other man's chest, he began punching him in the face. With each strike Ellington's flesh swelled and split open. Blood coated Santos's fists and still he couldn't stop. Someone grabbed his arm, but he shook him off. His rage was at himself for failing to keep Jane safe, at this sick twisted bastard who'd struck her beautiful face.

The sensation of a butterfly's wings touched his arm, and he caught a flash of pale blue out of the corner of his eye. And just like that, his rage evaporated leaving him feeling empty, exhausted. His head dropped forward, and his eyes closed.

"Santos, Santos can you hear me?"

The soft voice sounded as if it were miles away. Forcing himself to raise his head, he opened his eyes. Jane was crouched beside him, reaching for him. Her cool hands touched his face, his throat. Her beautiful blue eyes were watery and the concern on her face broke through the cocoon he'd built around his heart.

"Santos?"

"He hurt you." His voice was little more than a whisper. "He deserves to die."

"No, no, Santos. If you kill him then you will be taken away from me." Tears ran down her face. "Losing you will hurt me far worse than anything he could ever do."

"Jane—"

He started to rise, but his legs felt like overcooked spaghetti. Jane took his arm and eased it over her shoulders. She was so small beside him, and he was afraid to lean on her too much. He couldn't stand it if he hurt her more than she'd already—

"*Bien hecho, hermano.*" Antonio slipped under his other arm and threw his arm around Santos's waist. "Let me buy you a drink."

Santos began to laugh.

Chapter Seven

"I'm sorry I frightened you."

Santos's voice was a welcome rumble against her back.

"You have nothing to be sorry for." Rolling onto her back, she smiled up at him. "You saved me."

Rather than being pleased by her words, he became more remote. He made to leave her side.

"It was because of me that you were hurt in the first place."

"No, Santos. You can't think that way." She latched onto his uninjured arm. "You couldn't have known Peter would do something so insane."

"I never should've left you alone."

The anguish in his voice tore at her heart. There was no way she was going to let him take the fall for Peter's idiocy.

"I have news for you." She thumped him on the chest. "I'm a grown woman, and I make my own decisions. I chose to stay outside when you tried to convince me to come in."

"When he hit you, all I wanted to do was kill him." His eyes shone with unshed tears. "I was afraid I would lose you."

"And here I am, found again." She smiled. "You weren't the only one who wanted to kill him. I was scared, but I knew if I could delay him long enough that you and Antonio would find me."

The bedroom door opened, and Antonio came in.

"We have Giselle to thank." Santos nodded his head in his friend's direction. "She got mad at Antonio and told him Peter had taken you."

"But it was Santos who ran like the wind to get to you before Ellington could steal you away." Antonio joined them on the bed. "I never could keep up with him."

"I got shot." Santos snorted. "If you had kept up with me then chances are you would've had enough sense to dive for the gun."

"I don't know, your dive through the air was a thing of beauty..."

Jane released Santos and snuggled down between her two men. She wanted nothing more than to sleep for a day straight, but she didn't have that luxury. In only a few hours the sun would be up and she'd have to start packing to return home. Her fantasy weekend was almost over.

"What do you mean you didn't ask her?" Santos was saying.

"Me? I left her here with you. I thought you would ask her." Antonio shot back. "I was downstairs cleaning up your blood."

"Well I wouldn't have bled if you'd managed to keep up with me old man."

Santos shoved Antonio's shoulder and in the process jostled Jane.

"Hey, I'm here you know."

Both men looked at her.

"Still can't believe you didn't ask her," Antonio muttered.

"What, your vocal chords are frozen? You speak English as well as I."

"As well as me."

"That's what I said." Santos's eyes narrowed.

"No you didn't, you said 'as well as I' when 'as well as me' is correct."

"What the hell did you need to ask me?" she shouted.

Both men grinned, and she thought she saw a faint blush on Santos's cheeks.

"*Belleza,*" Antonio spoke. "We would like to ask you to continue this relationship beyond this weekend."

Her heart leapt.

"We would be honored if you would allow us to become not only your masters, but your partners."

Jane scrunched up her face and pretended to consider the situation.

"How long do I have to think about it?"

Santos looked stunned and the smile vanished from Antonio's face. They looked so crestfallen she began to laugh.

"I would be delighted to continue our current arrangement. Who knows where it might lead."

Antonio let out a whoop, and Santos kissed her on the cheek. Cuddled between them Jane thought of how lucky she was. She'd come here to test the sexual waters and instead she'd met two men who'd changed the rules in the middle of the game.

Watch out world, Beauty was ready to play.

About the Author

To learn more about Dominique Adair, please visit www.dominiqueadair.com. Send an email to Dominique at wilder@jcwilder.com or join her Yahoo! group to join in the fun with other readers as well as Dominique at http://groups.yahoo.com/group/thewilderside.

One hot man is good. Two's double the fun...
until your heart gets involved.

Tempt Me Twice

© 2009 Eden Bradley

Jessie has been in love with her bisexual best friend, Paul, since their college days. He's never made a move on her, though, and at this point she values his friendship too much to risk revealing her feelings. Especially since now he has a new male lover and seems so happy.

Paul and Noah have only Jessie's rest and relaxation in mind when they invite her along on a camping trip to Lake Tahoe. She's been pretty stressed out preparing to show her art at a major New York gallery. A weekend getaway will do her a world of good—and they won't take no for an answer.

Jesse thought she'd be nothing more than a third wheel on this trip. But Noah is as sweet and hot as Paul, and their first night turns into a heated tangle of bodies in the dark tent by the lake.

It's an erotic, intense experience that must come to an end. And when it does, will she still have her best friend?

Warning: Explicit and unusual sex in nearly every possible combination: boy on girl, boy on boy, boys on girl, with a little anal action and some spanking thrown in just to keep things interesting!

Born to protect women's hearts,
her own beats longingly for a mortal. Oops...

Oh Goddess

© 2009 Gwen Hayes

Ondina, one thousand years a goddess, doesn't think much of mortal men. Probably because her sole purpose in life is to protect the hearts of women who don't want to fall in love. And now one of those blasted men—Jack—has shattered her sacred chalice, trapping her in a mortal body.

Jackson Nichols, on the partner track at his law firm, is the first to admit he always follows his head. Never his heart. Dina is infuriating, messy, condescending, sexy, beautiful and...well, just about everything that doesn't fit into his meticulously planned life.

Neither expects to find many redeeming qualities in the other. But when push comes to love, which will Dina choose? Her newly human heart...or one thousand years of duty?

NOTE: All author and editor proceeds from the sale of *Oh Goddess* will be donated to the Coalition for Pulmonary Fibrosis. You can find out more about the foundation at www.coalitionforpf.org.

Warning: Recent studies show that consuming beverages while reading this story can cause damage to computer monitors, clothing, and sometimes nearby walls. Reader agrees to hold both Samhain Publishing Ltd. and Gwen Hayes harmless in case of accidental spewing caused by laughter.

My Bookstore & More
www.mybookstoreandmore.com
Green for the planet.
Great for your wallet.